SEALING THE DEAL

A BONDS OF MADNESS NOVEL

CATHERINE BANKS

I

POOR SOULS

CHAPTER ONE

You make one deal that doesn't have a happily ever after, and suddenly you get banished from the North Sea.

Had I known the little twit was a princess, I wouldn't have let the garbage-hoarding idiot sign it. Plus, her *daddy* should have taught her better about the consequences of magic. Everyone knows magic comes at a price. I explained to her in extreme detail that she would turn into sea foam.

I hardly thought it was fair that I got punished just because she couldn't use her womanly assets to charm the stupid human. Not having a voice shouldn't have been *that* big of a hindrance.

The king didn't care. I'd hurt his treasured baby girl, and he'd banished me. It took me months to find a new place to stay. I missed my old cave, but at least I had my faithful dog fish, Barnacle and Crustacean.

Barny and Crusty zipped around the cave, chasing each other. They desperately wanted to go out of the cave, but living in the Dead Sea required a bit of magic to protect us from the high salination.

It meant I had to make frequent trips out of the Dead Sea to get supplies for my spells, but I was okay with that. Back in the Atlantic I'd had frequent visitors and customers.

Now, it was just me and the dog fish. Oh, and my undead companions.

One of them shuffled into the cave carrying a wooden treasure chest.

"What do you have there, Blackleg?" I asked.

Blackleg had been a ruthless human pirate in his day. When I'd come to the Dead Sea, I'd found him and five of his crew mostly preserved inside of their sunken ship, and had resurrected them. They served me and did my bidding, which included searching for useful items along the sea floor. They weren't able to let sunlight touch them, so they stuck to shuffling along the floor of the ocean, chasing fish and scaring sharks now that they were mostly immortal.

He grunted, the only form of communication he was able to make, since fish had eaten his tongue, and opened the chest for me. Inside lay a myriad of jewels and coins.

I reached for one, and he snapped it closed, nearly catching my finger.

My gaze jerked up to his black, glowing orbs. "Excuse you."

He grunted and held out his hand.

I sighed. "Right. Payment. You damn pirates have no trust."

Not that I blamed him. His own crew had turned on him, killing him and sinking his ship once they'd stolen one from a navy.

On the far side of my cave sat a chest of drawers where I kept my most valuable items. Inside, I dug around until I found the item he craved most.

Once back in front of him, I held out the pair of gloves I'd sewn last week from the ship's mast he had brought me. Blackleg loved sharks, and wanted to pet them, but his bony hands kept scratching them instead. I gave him gloves so he

4

could pet them, but they only lasted a week at most before his bones tore holes in them, and he scratched the sharks, scaring them away again.

He put the gloves on, and his teeth clacked together in what I assumed was happiness, since he only did it when I gave him something he liked.

"Carry the chest to the storage room, please," I instructed him.

He grunted, picked up the chest, and carried it into one of the back rooms.

"I need to search for some supplies," I told Blackleg when he came back. "Can you and your men guard my cave?"

He nodded and sat on the ground, examining his gloved hands.

Blackleg had been a murderer, torturing men when he captured them, but he had never harmed women or children. I should have felt he got what he deserved, but I felt sad for him instead.

I would visit the human world on this trip and try to find some stronger material to make gloves for him so he could pet sharks more often.

"I should be gone for about a week," I said. "So, feel free to take turns watching the cave, so you can make a trip out to the sharks."

His teeth clacked together as he looked up at me.

I nodded, whistled to Barny and Crusty, and wrapped my cloak around my shoulders. The dog fish settled on my shoulders as I spun magic around the three of us, and walked out of the cave.

The salt content was so high that nothing could live here, which was why it was called the Dead Sea. My beautiful tentacles would have shriveled up in the water if I didn't have magic.

I used my tentacles to propel us through the water, headed

towards the passage I'd made beneath the land to connect the Dead Sea to the Mediterranean Sea. There were a couple islands that had a few supernatural creatures living on them, and beyond that was several countries of humans.

I preferred to avoid humans, but sometimes they were necessary, since they had the best trade.

I swam through the narrow tunnel I'd made, glad I had smeared bioluminescent goo along the walls to allow me to see a little bit. As I swam, I determined I should add more because it was still a bit claustrophobic for me.

Not that I cared if anyone else could use it, actually I preferred if no one entered this tunnel at all. But I wanted to be comfortable.

Once on the other side, I swam to the island Cyprus.

"Stay nearby and behave," I ordered Barny and Crusty.

They bobbed, brushed their scales against my face, and then zipped away to play.

I surfaced slowly, letting my eyes breach the water first, and then surveyed the shore.

A few harpies sat on the rocks, and when our eyes met, they shrieked at me.

I hissed and propelled myself upwards so they could see more of my body and a few of my tentacles.

They quieted, making room for me to climb onto the rocks and reach shore without touching me.

I nodded to them, and shifted into my human-like form, forcing my tentacles to disappear. I hated when I didn't have them, but they were really only useful in water anyway.

A few tree nymphs scurried out of my way as I walked towards the cave where the creatures met to sell their goods.

I smirked at the tree nymphs and continued on my way. At the entrance to the cave stood a cyclops. He was ten feet tall, at least, with a single eye that had a blue iris.

I saluted him.

He snarled and stepped back to let me enter. "Don't cause trouble," he growled after me.

I gasped and put a hand to my heart. "I would never."

He rolled his large eye and turned back around.

"*See* you later!" I called and laughed loudly as I headed into the cave. A quarter mile later, the cave opened into a large cavern. The cavern was filled with vendors, and creatures and beings of all kinds, including *humans*. I despised humans. They were filthy and horrible creatures.

I skirted around a human, my upper lip lifting in a snarl as I avoided touching them.

"Uschi," a deep voice called out.

I turned and smiled. "Hammerhead!" Hammerhead was man on land, but shark in the water. We got along very well, partly because we both hated that asshole in the Atlantic.

"What are you looking for today?" he asked, motioning at his supplies.

"Seaweed seeds and a few other items," I said and held out my list to him.

He examined the list and whistled. "Quite the assortment. Got a big spell planned?"

I shrugged and toyed with a jar of shriveled souls he kept on display. He refused to sell them, no matter what price I offered. "I like to keep well stocked in case something comes up."

"I don't have some of these, but Tomlin does. Give me twenty and I'll get you set up," he said.

I handed him my pouch of coins. "I'll wait here," I said and sat behind his items.

He nodded and headed over to another vendor, showing him my list and picking things up.

Less than ten minutes later, he had all of my items packaged in a backpack for me.

I tipped him extra. "Thank you."

"Are you headed to the human city?" he asked.

"Yes."

"Be careful. Rumor is that there are some shapeshifters over there causing trouble," he warned.

"Thanks for the warning. I'll let you know if I see anything or if there's any fun to be had," I promised and winked at him.

His laughter followed me out of the cave.

"Bye," I called to the cyclops as I left.

"Bye," he called back.

I headed across the island and then leapt into the sea. I whistled and started on my way, knowing Barny and Crusty would find me eventually.

Since I didn't have much to do, I opted to go a bit farther than normal and headed towards Rome.

Barny and Crusty swam around me, and then zipped off to have fun while I went to land.

The shores were empty, which made it easy for me to walk on land to the nearby town.

Normally, this town was lively, but tonight it was loud.

I headed to the pub and entered to find four gentlemen singing a drinking song at the top of their lungs.

They were handsome specimens with large muscles and strong jaws, and not human. They looked human at the moment, but I knew it was just one of their appearances. How? Magic.

I sat at the bar and ordered a drink from the bartender, who looked way more haggard than usual.

The men finished their song, and came to the bar to order another round.

They surrounded me on all sides.

"Hello, beautiful lady. When did you sneak in?" one of

them asked. He had long, dark, wavy hair that hung to his shoulders.

"While you were finishing your song," I answered and smiled at him.

"You're not from around here," one of the men with red hair said.

I smirked as I turned to look at him. "Neither are you boys."

"Where are you from?" a third one asked. This one had sandy-colored hair that covered one of his eyes.

"A bit far from here," I said. "You probably wouldn't know it."

"Try us," the first one said.

"Dead Sea," I answered.

They looked at each other and then at me.

"Nothing lives there," man number two said.

"Well, I'm not dead and I'm living in the Dead Sea," I replied.

"She's pulling our leg," the fourth one said. He had short hair, clipped very close to his ears. He had dark eyes that sparkled with mischief.

I shrugged. "You boys can think whatever you want."

"What's your name?" the third one asked, trying to move the hair out of his eyes.

I couldn't use my real name, because too many people knew what had happened in the Atlantic. So, I used my current name. "Uschi."

"Well, Uschi, are you up for a night of fun?" man three asked.

"I don't know if you boys can handle my type of fun," I teased, taking a big swig of my drink.

They all smiled, grinning ear to ear.

"Try us," man one taunted.

I raised my hands, gathered magic within them, and then let it explode outwards in a ring that spread throughout the bar. The humans froze a moment, and then pandemonium ensued while I laughed maniacally.

CHAPTER TWO

The humans began fighting, kissing, and screwing all around the room. Chairs went flying at the same time as clothes.

The four men around me surveyed my chaos, and then burst into laughter.

"You're more trouble than we are," man two said with a wide smile.

I drained the contents of my glass, left some coins on the bar top, and stood. "It was wonderful meeting you boys, but I really must be off."

"I thought you were going to have a night of fun with us," man four said with a pout.

A woman threw herself at him, trying to get his pants off.

I laughed and waved over my shoulder. "Have a good night, boys."

Once out of the bar, I cackled when I realized my magic had spread throughout the city.

"Whoops."

Picking my way through the crowd, I hopped into the ocean, and started my swim back home.

Crusty and Barny zipped next to me.

"Did you two have as much fun as me?" I asked, still chuck-ling about the mayhem.

They spun around me wildly, which meant they'd had fun, too.

"Good, let's go home."

We swam back to the Dead Sea, and I collapsed on the floor of my cave with an exaggerated sigh.

Blackleg stood from his spot and grunted once before walking out of the cave.

I waved my thanks to him and promptly fell asleep.

When I awoke later, I went to work making the gloves for Blackleg. I'd purchased a chainmail glove, and was working on attaching leather to the outside. That way, his bones wouldn't pierce the chainmail, and the leather would be soft on the sharks he wanted to pet.

Halfway through the day, I felt a disturbance in the waters.

Peeking out, I stared in disbelief at a boat on the water. Who sailed on the Dead Sea?

"Uschi!" a familiar male voice called.

The men from last night?

I swam up to the bottom of their boat, eavesdropping.

"I'm telling you, she isn't here. She lied," another familiar male voice said.

I peeked my head out from under the boat, and man two screamed.

Laughter bubbled out of me.

He glared at me, and then three more heads turned to look at me.

"What are you four doing here?" I asked, glad I was able to hide my lower body beneath their boat. Most were put off by tentacles.

"We need your help," man one said.

I arched a brow. "My help?"

"We were sent to find a woman, but we can't find her. We thought you could help us," man three said.

My body tensed. "What woman?"

"We can't tell you more until you agree to help," man four said.

"I don't help find lost people," I said. "Wrong type of witch."

I used magic to alter my lower body into a human-looking one, and dove down towards my cave.

There was a splash behind me, and I gaped in disbelief at a seal floundering in the water.

What was that idiot doing? He couldn't survive in this water!

He tried to surface, but his eyes rolled into the back of his head.

The other three stood on the boat, yelling.

Selkies! That explained a lot.

I grabbed the stupid seal, swam him to the shore, sliding his body on the sand, and then climbed out and began healing him. Luckily, it was dark, and there were no humans nearby.

The seal turned into man one, and he gasped for air. "How can you swim in that?"

"Magic, you idiot," I grumbled and finished healing him.

The other three rowed their boat over and climbed out.

"I told you not to jump in," man four said with a frown.

"We will pay you whatever you want," man two said.

"Why is it so important that you find this person? Is she your lover? Maybe she ran away and doesn't want to come back." I moved away from them now that man one was healed.

"She is an important person. If we don't find her, we will remain cursed the rest of our lives," man one said.

"Conall!" man four yelled. "Why are you telling her that?"

"She saved my life. The least we can do is be honest," man one, aka Conall, said.

Well, at least they weren't hunting me down. "Does this have anything to do with the ruler of the sea of the Atlantic?" I asked.

"No," Conall furrowed his brows. "Why?"

"I'm not fond of him," I said with a smile. "Fine, who are we looking for?"

"Amphitrite," man three answered.

I laughed and shook my head. "Poseidon's wife? You ever think she ran away because he is an overbearing—"

Four hands covered my mouth.

"I wouldn't speak ill of him so close to the water," Conall said.

These boys had no idea about my past with Poseidon. That worked in my favor.

"Fine," I agreed. "I will help you."

"Your price?" man four asked, narrowing his eyes at me.

"I get to return her to Poseidon with you. I want him to know it was me who helped find her," I said.

The boys exchanged glances and then walked several feet away to talk in a quiet circle.

They talked for several minutes, arguing back and forth.

I sat on the beach, enjoying the breeze as I stared up at the stars overhead. I didn't often take time to enjoy the stars.

"In exchange for your help, we will allow you to return her to Poseidon with us," Conall said.

I held out my hand. "Deal."

Conall looked at his friends before finally reaching forward and shaking my hand. Magic zapped our hands, and he jerked his away.

"What was that?" man four asked, growling.

I lifted a brow at him. "Magic. You made a binding agreement with me."

"You didn't tell us that would happen," man two snapped.

I put my hands on my hips. "You sought out a witch, to help you with a quest to break a curse, and didn't think I'd have some type of insurance policy?"

"What happens to Conall if we break it?" man three asked.

"You're all bound to the agreement by your shared curse." I smirked. "And, nothing too bad happens. You're just cursed to become my undead slaves."

"What!" Conall shrieked.

I doubled over as I laughed. "Your faces! Oh, man!" I straightened and wiped my eyes. "You'll be marked as oath breakers. Just a tattoo. Nothing else. I'm not evil." Despite what Triton thought.

They all relaxed, but their glares remained.

I folded my arms across my chest. "Planning to break your deal? Why make it if you weren't going to go through with it?"

"We'll hold up our end of the bargain," Conall said.

"I need to pack. Give me an hour." I dusted the sand from my rear.

"We can come with you," Conall offered.

I smirked. "Sorry, but my place is secret. Don't fret, boys. I'll be back." Without waiting for their arguments, I jumped into the sea and sped towards home.

"Blackleg!" I called as I packed a bag. "Blackleg!"

The undead pirate grunted from behind me.

I spun and said, "I'm going to be gone for a long time. I need you to hold down the fort and keep and eye on Barnacle and Crustacean, okay?"

He bobbed his head once.

I held out the new gloves, and his eye sockets widened. He gingerly took them from me, examining them.

"They should hold up while I'm gone. Try not to be too rough on them, though. Okay?"

He bobbed his head and petted the gloves. Had he been alive with eyes and tear ducts, I bet he would have shed a tear or two.

"Don't let anyone find my cave. You understand?"

He gave me a glare, which was a feat since he had no eyeballs.

I nodded and slung my bag over my shoulder. "Don't forget to feed the fish every day."

He grunted and slid his new gloves on, flexing his hands and admiring them.

I left with a smile on my face and surfaced in human form.

The guys turned to look at me.

"Alright, where to first?" I asked.

"We heard there was a black market on Cyprus," Conall said. "You know of it?"

I nodded. "I frequent it, but I don't think I'll be able to take you four in."

"Why not?" man four asked with a scowl.

"First, what are your names? I've assigned you numbers, but that's tiresome."

"Conall," Conall said with a smirk.

I rolled my eyes.

"Marrok," man two said.

"Phelan," man three said.

"Wolfram," man four said.

They were pretty fitting names. Especially, Wolfram's.

"Alright, instead of going over land, I'll take you through my tunnel. It's faster, and I won't have to deal with humans," I said.

"We can't swim in that water," Wolfram snapped.

I gave him a look, letting him know that I didn't appreciate him insinuating I was an idiot. I wiggled my fingers. "Magic, Wolfie. Magic. Now, come on. Shift."

They looked at each other, then at me, and then back at each other.

I sighed and turned my back. "Better?"

I felt the magic stir behind me, and when I turned, four seals blinked up at me.

"You four are so adorable!" I gushed, reaching over to pat Conall on the head.

Phelan barked angrily.

I stuck my tongue out at him and walked in the water. "Hurry, stay at my side. I'll create a bubble to shield us from the salt."

They scurried after me and I had to refrain from gushing or baby talking to them.

Once all four were next to me, I created the shield and jumped into the water. They followed closely, staying within touching distance.

I set my hand on Conall's back and pointed at the tunnel. "That way."

He took off, and I held onto his back, letting him pull me along instead of shifting back into my cecaelia form. I loved my tentacles, but for some reason, I felt it was better to hide them for now.

"Just to the right," I said, guiding Conall.

We entered the cave, and the seals crowded closer to me.

Were they scared of the darkness? Or were they worried I would try to separate them?

Both were possible, but I felt like the latter was most likely the reason.

We emerged from the cave into the sea, and I directed Conall to the island.

The harpies hissed at us, and the seals cowered a bit.

I hissed back at the harpies, letting some of my magic flare, and they shrank away, resorting to glares.

The guys switched forms.

"Why are the harpies afraid of you?" Marrok asked.

"Because they know I'm stronger than them," I said with a shrug. "Come on, let's see if we can get you guys in. If not, I'll just have to find the information for us."

"You're not going in without at least one of us," Wolfram growled.

"Down, boy," I ordered. "I don't take kindly to orders."

"Let's just see if we can all get in," Conall said, trying to defuse the situation.

We approached the cyclops, who glared down at the guys. "What's this?" he asked me.

"They've come to barter for information," I said.

"You claiming responsibility?" he asked, turning his eye on me.

I sighed. "That sounds like a bad idea."

"They do anything wrong, and you'll be banned," he said.

"Don't threaten me," I snapped.

The cyclops took an involuntary step back, growled when he realized it, and then said, "Go on. Don't cause trouble or I'll toss you out."

"You'll try," I muttered beneath my breath as we walked in.

"Don't tempt me," he murmured.

I growled and waved at the guys. "Hurry up." I had a bad feeling about this, and I'd only just left my cave. These boys were hiding something, and were prone to trouble. Even the cyclops could sense it.

I was so doomed.

CHAPTER THREE

"Uschi!" Hammerhead called. "What are you doing back here so soon?"

I smiled as I approached him, but his smile disappeared when he saw the guys behind me.

"What's this? You get yourself a harem?" he asked.

"Fuck no," Wolfram gagged.

My fingers twitched to turn him into a sea slug, but I curled them into a fist instead.

"They need information. I'm just their babysitter," I said with a smile. "Help me out?"

"You paying?" he asked.

I shook my head. "No, they are."

"Two hundred," he told the boys.

"You don't even know what we're going to ask. You have no idea if you know what we want or not." Marrok frowned.

"Just give him the two hundred," I said with a sigh and shook my head. These boys were such amateurs. Why would Poseidon send them after Amphitrite?

Conall handed Hammerhead the two hundred and then stepped back beside me.

I wouldn't tell him, but I enjoyed his presence. It had been a long time since I'd had a man stand so close to me.

"She's on an island to the west," Hammerhead said. "She's stuck and needs help getting off the island."

"Creature?" I asked.

He glanced at me, our eyes locking, and after a moment he sighed. "Gorgon."

Medusa. Dammit.

"I hate fighting gorgons," I grumbled.

"You're going with them?" Hammerhead asked, eyes wide.

"How did you know what we were going to ask about?" Wolfram demanded, stepping closer to Hammerhead.

I grabbed Wolfram's shirt and pushed him back. "Don't start a fight you can't win, idiot."

"It's my job to know things. Uschi, why are you working with these idiots?"

"They offered something I couldn't resist," I said with a smirk.

"This has to do with Poseidon, doesn't it?" Hammerhead asked, smirking himself.

I glared at him. "Quiet."

"You have a past with Poseidon?" Conall asked.

Hammerhead burst into laughter, the sound bouncing around the cave. "Oh, Uschi! You tricky woman you. Boys, I want you to know something. This is free of charge—"

"Hammerhead," I growled, taking a step closer.

"Uschi is one of the most powerful witches I've ever met. Don't think you can get one over on her or that you'll ever be able to defeat her. Also, if you get the chance, try to convince her to be your mate. She's one of the best there is. You won't find a better option for a mate."

I stared at Hammerhead, blinking in silent disbelief.

Hammerhead smirked. "Don't think that I don't know who you really are, Uschi. Remember, it's my job to know things."

Well, crap.

"How much do I have to pay you to keep that secret?" I asked tersely.

He bent forward to whisper in my ear.

Conall took a step closer, which made me smile despite the situation.

Hammerhead whispered in my ear, "One kiss, and I'll keep your secret until we both die."

I held out my hand, and he shook it immediately.

Then, Hammerhead pulled me forward, dipped me sideways, and kissed me deeply.

My head spun with the kiss, and I kissed him back before I realized what I was doing. He righted me and stepped back.

"Worth it," he panted and then walked away laughing.

"Well, now that that's taken care of, we should buy some supplies for gorgon hunting." I smoothed down my hair and turned to face the guys. They were all glaring at Hammerhead's retreating back.

"Why would you kiss him?" Conall asked.

"It's a minor price for him to keep my secrets," I said with a shrug as I started towards the market.

"Who are you really?" Wolfram asked as they followed me.

I smirked. "Do you think I would have just kissed a sharkman to keep that secret if I was just going to tell you?" I patted his head. "I know you're smarter than that, Wolfie."

"Wolfram," he growled. "My name is Wolfram."

I waved and headed over to one of the vendors who I knew had the items I needed.

She was an old lamia who had been attacked by a gorgon when she was young. It had created a permanent hatred in her.

"Hello, Lansa," I greeted and bowed.

She bowed back. "Uschi. What brings you to my table?"

"Gorgon hunting," I said and smiled.

She returned my smile, but there was no warmth there. "Wonderful. What's your budget?"

"Boys?" I asked, turning to them.

"One hundred," Conall answered.

She scoffed. "For five of you?"

"Yes," I nodded.

"I just need fifty and for you to bring me back one of her snakes," Lansa said.

I beamed. "Done."

She held out her hand, and I shook it. "If I die—"

She nodded. "Our deal is null and void. Yes."

Conall handed me the money, and I handed it to her. She began gathering weapons and magic potions, stacking them on the ground in five piles for us.

"Isn't that rather cheap?" Phelan whispered in my ear.

I shivered at his breath sliding along my earlobe and nodded. "Yes, but it's because she despises them. Us killing one is a happy day for her."

He didn't respond, which was probably for the best since Lansa could hear everything that we said.

"Uschi," she called as she finished the piles.

I walked to her. "Yes?"

"Be careful with them. There's something not right with that group," she whispered.

I bowed. "Thank you for your advice. I can feel it, too. I'm fairly certain it has to do with their curse, but I haven't been able to pinpoint it yet."

"If they kill you, may I seek revenge?" she asked.

"I've claimed dibs on that," Hammerhead said, approaching us.

Lansa sighed. "He always claims dibs on the fun jobs. Fine, but if you die, I get to seek revenge for her death."

Hammerhead chuckled. "Deal."

They shook, and I felt fear for the first time. "Is my death so certain?"

"No," Lansa answered immediately. "However, better prepared than not. Plus, I think they look rather tasty." She licked her lips and then let her tongue flicked out in a snake-like fashion as she tasted the air.

"You can't eat them unless they betray me," I ordered her.

She pouted. "You're no fun."

"Are we ready?" Wolfram asked, coming up to us.

"Yes," I said and smiled. "We're all set."

"Uschi, a moment?" Hammerhead asked.

I followed him a bit away, keeping an eye on the guys as they picked up the items from Lansa, and she explained what they were. The guys kept glancing at Hammerhead and me.

"What?" I asked him.

"Poseidon hasn't been himself lately," Hammerhead whispered. "This could be a trap."

I looked up at him with an arched brow. "What would he want to trap me for? Our past is in the past. He has a wife who is better suited for him."

"She ran away. The reason is unknown."

"Even to you?" I asked with wide eyes.

He nodded. "Even to me."

Well, shit.

"What is this information going to cost me?" I asked him, hands on my hips. "I haven't had a customer in a while, so I don't have much money."

"Just, stay alive and come back," he said.

"Hammerhead, you almost sound like you care. Are you ill?" I reached a hand out and touched his head.

He smirked and kissed the back of my hand. His smirk left and he stared down at me. "Uschi, I mean it. Don't let them trick you. Stay alive and come back."

My heart beat faster, and I nodded. "Will do."

He looked down at my human legs. "And, keep your tentacles hidden. I don't think they should know who you really are."

I smirked. "I'm not a fool, Hammerhead. I know."

He nodded and kissed my cheek. "Two of them are rather jealous of me touching you. If I were you, I'd bed them quick and claim them as yours. That way, Poseidon can't use them to kill you."

"If I claim them, he'll definitely try to use them against me," I grumbled.

He chuckled. "You may be right, but I have the feeling claiming them might be the best course of action."

I looked over at the guys, who were now all staring at me and Hammerhead. They were attractive, and I wouldn't mind having a harem of selkies.

"I'll consider it."

He nodded, kissed my cheek again, and left.

Conall and Marrok walked to me.

"Are you ready?" I asked them.

"Is he your lover?" Marrok asked.

I laughed loudly and shook my head. "No."

"Then why was he touching you?" Conall asked.

"Because I have no lover. I'm allowed to let men touch me. Does it bother you to see a man touch a woman? Are you into men?" I asked, tilting my head to the side as I looked at them.

"No, we just don't like when men overstep their boundaries and touch women who don't want to be touched," Conall said.

I smiled. "Boys, if I didn't want him to touch me, he wouldn't have. I appreciate your concern, but I can handle myself." I patted them both on the cheek as I walked by, and bowed to Lansa again. "Thank you for your assistance."

"A snake," she reminded me. "Or two."

"I'll bring you as many as I can," I said with a laugh.

She smiled. "Bringing me one of those boys back wouldn't hurt either."

I laughed and shook my head. "I'm not letting you eat them, Lansa."

She sighed. "Spoilsport."

I bowed and she bowed back, and then I headed towards the cave's exit.

"Stop right there!" a deep voice shouted.

We were so close! I knew it had been too good to think we could escape without trouble.

I turned, and the boys turned with me, forming a wall of man flesh between me and the one yelling.

"What do you want?" Wolfram asked.

"I know who you are," the guy growled. "There's a bounty on your head. I'm here to claim it."

Shit.

He opened his mouth. "You're U—"

I hit him with my magic, freezing his vocal chords, and making him fall to his knees.

I pushed through the guys, grabbed the idiot by his throat and said, "Your voice belongs to me now."

His mouth gaped open and closed as he tried to talk.

I pulled out the shell I kept voices in, and added his to it. "If you even so much as write my name down, you'll burst into a million pieces. So, forget my name, now."

I hid the shell again, so the guys wouldn't see it, and turned, walking back to them.

Marrok and Conall's eyes widened at the same time that I heard the ground shift behind me as the man ran for me.

I ducked, prepared to fight, but Marrok and Conall were suddenly beside me, and punching the guy in the face.

The guy flew backwards, knocking over Plark, a crotchety old satyr. Plark roared, hit the guy, and then turned towards us, raising his sword in the guys' direction. "You!"

"Time to go!" I shouted, grabbed Marrok and Conall by the hands, and raced towards the exit.

We flew past the cyclops and towards the water.

"Get them!" Plark yelled.

"He started it!" I yelled over my shoulder at Plark. "Don't blame the boys."

"I told you not to cause trouble!" the cyclops yelled.

I shrugged, smiling wide, and dove into the water with the guys right next to me.

We didn't surface for several miles, and then I turned and smiled at them. "I knew you guys were trouble."

"You started it," Wolfram growled.

"Technically, that guy started it when he yelled at her," Conall countered.

"Let's get food," I said and swam towards the nearest continent.

"There are humans there," Conall reminded me.

"Which means food," I said and rolled my eyes. "Duh."

CHAPTER FOUR

THE FOOD WAS DELICIOUS, AND WE BURNED OFF THE calories from our dessert as we ran for the docks and stole a ship. They'd decided they didn't want to swim the entire way, and I was fine with that.

I stood on the mermaid figurehead at the prow of the ship, letting the wind blow my hair around. The sea always smelled better when I was above it.

"So, you're pretty famous, huh?" Marrok asked from behind me.

I turned, facing him. "A bit." I jumped down to the ship's deck, and ran my fingers over the railing.

"You don't look happy about it," he commented.

I scoffed. "No. I wish my name was never known. Kings care not for peons desires, though."

"What happened?" he asked softly, stepping closer to me.

I shook my head and moved away. "I don't want to discuss it."

"We aren't your enemies," he whispered.

"Not yet," I whispered too softly for him to hear.

I was furious that someone had put a bounty out on my head. Who could it have been?

Triton despised me, but I had left the Atlantic at his order. Had the grief gotten to him and now he wanted me dead?

If it was him, I would march back to his castle and rip that trident from his dead hands.

"I didn't mean to upset you," Marrok said. "I just want to learn more about you."

I turned to face him, hands on my hips. "Why? Once we've captured Poseidon's run away bride and returned her, you'll never see me again."

He scowled. "Uschi, it's not like—"

"Witch!" Wolfram yelled. "Where is this island?"

I cringed, hating being referred to in that way. That was how Triton had always called me.

"My name is Uschi," I growled as I headed towards him.

He held out a map without another word.

I pushed it away. "It's not on there."

"Every island is on here," he growled.

I looked at it and shook my head. "No, it's not."

All four guys clustered around the map, scowling down at it.

"Are you brothers?" I asked.

"Yes," they all answered simultaneously.

"Half-brothers," Conall added.

"You're demigods!" I gasped, realizing why I was attracted to them. I backed up a few steps. "Who is your father?"

"You wouldn't know him," Wolfram grumbled and handed the map to Phelan. "How do we find the island if it isn't on a map?"

I smiled. "You don't. The island finds you."

He growled and marched towards me with his fists curled. "If you are trying to sabotage us—"

I held my ground, not the least bit frightened of him. "I'm telling you the truth."

Wolfram towered over me, glaring and trying to intimidate me.

Before he could react, I bounced up on my toes and pressed my lips to his, and then darted back.

His mouth gaped open and his eyes widened, the anger completely gone.

"The island will show itself to me. I will find Amphitrite, and we will return her to Poseidon." I turned and walked to the prow of the ship, looking out over the water. I understood why they didn't trust me. I wouldn't have trusted me either. But they would have to trust me to find the island. I didn't think the island would show for them.

The guys left me alone the rest of the night, which suited me just fine.

Something moved in the water ahead of us with a familiar shine.

"Oh, shit. Boys!" I yelled and ran towards the guys. "Plug your ears!" I screamed.

They turned and looked at me.

"What?" Marrok asked.

"Plug your ears! Now!" I screamed, sliding to a stop next to them. I started weaving a spell, but it was too late.

Female voices began singing a song of seduction. I knew though, that it was also a song of death.

The guys turned towards the front of the boat, and started walking.

"Dammit! You idiots. Why won't you just listen to me," I growled at them. I ran to the side and grabbed rope. It wasn't going to be easy, but I had to secure them to the mast before they jumped over.

I tackled Conall, who was the closest to the prow, and he laughed.

Laughter was not what I had expected. I started trying to tie him up, but he rolled over and smiled at me. "It's okay. You don't have to tie us up," he said.

I looked at the other guys, and found them all smiling at me. "What?" I gaped.

"We're selkies. We are of the sea. They can't lure us into the sea and drown us," Marrok explained.

I relaxed, but then realized I was still sitting on Conall's lap. Rolling away, I sat on the deck and stared at them. "You're immune to the sirens' call?"

They all nodded.

I fell onto my back and stared up at the moon overhead. "That would have been nice to know before I started freaking out," I muttered.

"Little demigods, come play with us," one of the sirens called.

I stood and headed to the railing, glaring down at the three sirens: Ligeia, Molpe, and Raidne.

They hissed, showing off their shark-like teeth.

"What are you doing here, sea witch?" Ligeia asked.

"These men are not going to come to you. Beat it. Go find some humans to devour," I growled.

"They aren't yours," Molpe hissed.

I smirked. "Did I say they were?"

"They'll never claim you. They'll never let you claim them," Ligeia said.

I shrugged, but didn't respond because the statements actually hurt my feelings. She was right.

"It really bothers me when people speak on my behalf," Wolfram growled down at the sirens. I hadn't heard him come up to my side. "Leave. You're not going to lure us in, except to come and kill you."

They hissed again, giving me one last glare before diving back down into the deep.

I should have let it go. I should have turned and went to the prow again, but I was too upset.

I dove overboard, ignoring the guys' calls, and chased after the sirens.

"What do you want, sea witch?" Molpe asked.

"You insulted me. I can't let that stand," I said. I used my magic to transform into a shark, and leapt at the closest siren.

They screamed as I killed them, their blood clouding the water. It wasn't as satisfying as I thought it would be, but I did feel better. I shifted back and swam to the ship, gripping the side as I looked up at the four sets of eyes staring at me.

"A little help?" I asked and held up my hand.

"They were leaving," Conall said, brows furrowed.

Wolfram leaned over and grasped my wrist, hauling me up onto the ship.

Once my feet were on the deck, I answered him. "They insulted me. I couldn't let that stand."

"You didn't have to kill them. You could have hurt them and —" Conall began.

Strangely, it was Wolfram who cut him off. "If she shows mercy to them, the others will think she is weak. She can't appear weak to any of them. Not in this sea."

He was right. Why did the jerk have to be the one who understood me?

I returned to the figurehead, waiting for the island to show itself.

The night turned to day and with it came a heat I despised. I lay on the deck, arm over my face, panting.

"Want me to throw a bucket of water on you?" Marrok asked.

"Please," I begged.

He chuckled. "I was teasing."

"Is it always this hot up here?" I groaned, rolled onto my side, and dropped my arm so I could see him.

"You stay underwater a lot?" he asked.

I nodded. "I have a cave."

"Is your mate there now?"

"I told you, I don't have a mate," I said and rolled onto my back again, closing my eyes.

"Why not?"

"Sea witch, remember?"

"So?"

I rolled my head over to look at him. "I'm scary powerful. Men don't like powerful women. Even less so when they're as powerful as I am."

"You've been hanging out with the wrong guys," Marrok said with a chuckle.

"You're not wrong," I muttered.

"Where did you live before? That guy said there was a bounty out for your head."

"Probably some unsatisfied customer. It's not my fault they don't read the contract. I give it to them, and they just sign away."

"Are you ever going to trust us enough to tell us who you really are?" he asked.

He looked curious instead of angry, which surprised me.

"I'll reveal my true self when we go to Poseidon," I promised.

His brows furrowed. "You really don't trust us, do you?"

"No offense, but we don't know each other. You could be planning to turn me in for that bounty for all I know. Or maybe

Poseidon sent you to get me and his runaway bride. I never trust anything when gods are involved.

"I understand that," he said with a chuckle and lay on his back beside me on the deck. "The gods are tricky assholes."

"Who cursed you?" I asked.

"Poseidon," he answered immediately. "If we don't return his queen, we forever stay cursed."

"You're a selkie by blood, so that's not the curse. What is?" I could feel the curse on them, but not what it did.

"It's complicated," he mumbled.

In other words, he didn't want to tell me.

"Okay," I said, deciding not to pry. Not yet anyway. I would pry more later.

Conall laid down on my other side. "Is this a nap party?" he asked.

"This is a whining party," I said.

"What are we whining about today?" he asked.

I didn't need to look at him to know he was smirking.

"Being hot," I said in the whiniest voice possible.

"You're mad that you're hot? I've never heard a woman complain about being attractive before."

I rolled my head to look at him. "I meant physically."

"Me, too." His grin widened and he gave me a slow once over, as well as he could lying down.

My lips ticked up into a smile. "You're just flirting because I saved your life."

"Am not."

A cold splash of water rained down on me. I gasped and wiped my face.

Wolfram stood over me with an empty bucket. "There," he said, scowling. Did he ever not scowl?

I smiled up at him. "You're so considerate. Thanks, Wolfie."

He grumbled something beneath his breath and stomped away.

I sighed and relaxed. "Much better."

"We could tie you to the ship and drag you behind us," Phelan offered.

That actually wasn't a bad idea. Maybe the island would show up faster.

"No," Marrok and Conall said at the same time.

I sighed. "You two are no fun."

"She turned into a shark, remember?" Phelan said.

"What else can you turn into?" Conall asked.

I winked at him. "That's a secret."

Phelan scoffed and rolled his eyes.

My body began tingling, and fear washed over me. I dashed to the stairs and ran below deck. That feeling meant only one thing. A god.

Moments later, a deep voice asked, "What have you learned so far about my wife?"

Poseidon.

Conall peeked down at me from the deck.

I waved my hand in a shooing motion, and then tried to conceal my magic as well as I could. If Poseidon knew I was here, he would blow my cover straight to the Underworld.

"We had a few tips, but so far they haven't proven fruitful," Wolfram said.

He was lying to Poseidon. Why? He could have told him about the island.

"You have less than a week until your time is up," Poseidon snapped. "Find her and bring her to me, or you'll never enjoy the touch of a woman again."

Oh! That prick! How dare he do something like that to those boys. Wait. What had they done to deserve that punishment?

Wolfram walked down the stairs first, and the others followed.

"He's gone," Wolfram told me. "You can stop hiding."

"What did you do to make him curse you?" I asked.

"Tell us why you're hiding," Phelan countered.

"I have history with him. We don't get along. If he saw me with you, he might decide your agreement was off or try to kill us." Answering honestly felt like the best option.

"We slept with his daughter," Wolfram said. "It was consensual, but he didn't believe that his baby girl would screw four guys at once."

Well, well. Didn't they just become even more enticing?

"You lied to him," I said, lifting a brow.

"Not really. So far, we haven't seen the island. So, it wasn't a lie." Wolfram shrugged.

"You didn't tell him I was here."

"You bolted for the stairs like you were on fire. I assumed you didn't want him knowing you were here. We have our own issues with gods, so I understand," he said.

Was that compassion I heard?

I smirked. "Careful, Wolfram. You're starting to make me like you."

CHAPTER FIVE

"THERE!" I YELLED, POINTING TOWARDS STARBOARD. "THE island!"

Wolfram ran to the wheel while the others ran to me.

Conall grabbed my hand, pulling me back to the deck.

"Is there a place to dock?" Wolfram asked.

"No, we will have to drop anchor and take a rowboat in," I said, heading towards the boat on the side.

"Just wait until we drop anchor," Marrok said and grabbed my wrist.

Dark tendrils of power shot out of me towards him, but I managed to stop them before they touched him.

"Please, don't snatch my wrist like that," I whispered, making the tendrils disappear.

He released my wrist. "I'm sorry. I didn't mean to startle you."

I smiled at him, trying to lighten the mood. "It's okay. I just like your head where it is. I'd hate for it to be removed over a misunderstanding."

"I think you like more than my head," he replied with a smirk.

I almost sagged in relief at his playful response.

"Drop anchor," Wolfram ordered.

Conall pushed the anchor off the ship and then joined us by the row boat.

The anchor hit the seabed, and the ship halted.

The guys worked together to lower the row boat and hopped down into it.

"Maybe I should stay with the boat," I offered.

"Uschi, come on," Conall called.

"We aren't leaving you alone with the boat," Wolfram said.

"Afraid I might steal it?" I asked, a hand on my hip.

He smirked. "No. But I have a feeling we're going to need your help on the island. We've never fought a gorgon before."

I chewed on my lower lip, debating. I was certain Amphitrite wouldn't be happy to see me.

"Jump. I'll catch you," Marrok said.

With a sigh, I jumped over the railing.

As promised, Marrok caught me and then sat down with me in his lap. I blinked in shock, looking from him to the others, but they were acting like it was normal for me to sit on his lap.

Okay. I could play along, too.

I leaned my head on his shoulder and closed my eyes. Part of me longed to jump into the sea, but I held that feeling at bay. I needed to be human for a bit longer.

Marrok turned his head and whispered in my ear, "Were I not cursed, this situation would be a lot different."

I chuckled, and then stifled the laughter. "Are you trying to sweet talk me in hopes that I'll keep you alive?"

"No, just stating the obvious. If I could, I would screw you until you passed out from bliss," he growled in my ear.

Oh, gods.

"Would you share me with your brothers?" I asked.

37

"Not the first time. The first time, it will just be you and me," he whispered, his voice hoarse.

And, my panties were soaked.

"You sound confident that I would sleep with you," I said.

His hand slid around my waist, sliding my shirt up so he could touch my skin. "You want to. I see the way you look at us. Like we are just fresh meat for the taking."

I laughed, unable to hold it in.

"Are you going to help row at all?" Phelan asked.

I sighed. "Fine."

I stood, weaved magic between my fingers, and then blew it behind us. The row boat lurched forward and zipped towards the island.

The guys gripped the boat, and Marrok yanked me down into his lap again.

I slowed the boat so it gently slid into the beach, extricated myself from Marrok's hold, and hopped into the island.

The guys climbed out, expressionless.

I examined the island before us. To the left was a volcano. To the right, mountains and a jungle mingled together.

Where would I hide a sea queen?

"Volcano," I said and headed towards it.

"Why there?" Conall asked.

"You steal the sea god's wife. Where would you take her? Somewhere the God would be weakened, like a place full of molten rock. Plus, snakes like hot places."

"Makes sense to me," Marrok said with a shrug.

Wolfram waved. "Lead the way."

I paused and decided that altering my appearance might be the best approach. "One minute," I said. With a loud pop, my body transformed into a light-skinned, blonde haired woman. I started walking and heard the guys grumbling behind me.

"What?" I asked, glancing over my shoulder.

"We preferred the other form," Marrok answered, coming up to walk beside me.

I smiled. "Don't worry, this is only temporary." Their compliment shouldn't have made me so happy, but I let the warmth flow through me. Soon enough, they would find out my true identity and abandon me.

Then it would just be me, my dog fish, and Blackleg.

We headed into the jungle which blocked the way to the volcano. Marrok pushed vines and branches out of the way for me.

I hadn't had a man do something so considerate for me in a very long time.

Dropping my head, I continued along the path silently. The guys made small talk, but I ignored it.

"Uschi," Phelan said.

I looked up at him. "Hm?"

"What's wrong? Do you sense something? You haven't said a word in an hour, which is definitely a record."

Resisting the urge to smile, I said, "It's nothing to worry about. I don't sense anything. I'm just thinking."

"Thinking about what?" Conall asked.

I blew out a breath, but didn't respond. These guys sure were nosey for a group that withheld lots of information.

"Come on," Conall urged.

"Just thinking about what I'll be doing after we return Amphitrite and we go our separate ways," I said, which was partly true.

"Aw, you're going to miss us, aren't you?" Wolfram teased.

I didn't respond because I would. What the hell? I didn't know these guys. How had they wormed their way into my brain so easily?

"I'll be going to the nearest town to add a dozen or so

notches to my belt once we are done with Poseidon," Phelan said, giving a lewd smile in my direction.

Was he trying to bait me?

"I'm sure you'll make stops at several cities," I said, smiling wide like it didn't bother me.

His smile slipped away and a scowl replaced it.

A branch snapped ahead, and I held up my hand, stopping and getting them to stop, too.

We listened, but there was no more movement.

I crept forward, slowly pushing a branch aside to peek through.

Taloned hands grabbed me, jerking me against a scaled body, and slitted pupils met mine.

I tried to break free, but she stared into my eyes, freezing me in place.

"Uschi!" Conall yelled.

The gorgon fled into the trees, carrying me with her.

Well, crap. I didn't see this happening.

She carried me through the jungle, moving through the trees gracefully. Once through the trees, she went into the hills just before the volcano, into a cave that was difficult to spot.

It was hopeless. The guys would never find me. I just needed to figure out a way to break her spell with one of my own.

She slid through the tunnels, her scaled body hissing along the stone ground. The farther we went, the hotter it got. My skin broke out into a sweat so fierce, it drenched my clothes.

Finally, she set me down. Before me was another frozen person, a woman.

Amphitrite!

Her eyes met mine, and I could see the surprise in them. Did she recognize me even in my disguise?

"Who are you and why are you here?" the gorgon hissed at me.

Her spell lifted, and I struck her with my own power, right in the chest.

She hissed and slid backwards a bit.

"You messed with the wrong person," I growled.

"Who are you and why are you here?" the gorgon asked again.

"I have many names, but currently go by Uschi. I am here to return your prisoner to her rightful place," I said.

"She is mine. I found her wandering and lost. She did not even try to flee when I found her," the gorgon said.

"You don't know who she is, do you?" I asked and laughed maniacally.

"What?" the gorgon asked.

"That's Poseidon's wife! You idiot. Let me return her, and we can part with no bloodshed," I offered.

The gorgon's eyes widened, and the snakes on her head hissed.

"Let me keep one of the boys you brought with you," the gorgon said, trying to barter.

"They aren't for sale," I said and shook my head. "They don't belong to me, anyway."

"So, you won't mind if I keep them?" she asked, smiling. Her tongue flicked out, tasting the air.

"As I said, they aren't mine," I shrugged. "I am here for Amphitrite. Let me have her and you can do what you want."

"That hurts," Wolfram said. "And here I thought we might have something."

I spun around, eyes wide.

Shit. How had they found me so quickly?

The gorgon started to move towards them, but I grabbed her arm, dodging a few of the snakes that tried to bite me.

"Release your spell on the sea queen," I ordered her.

She hissed, but did so.

Amphitrite slumped to the ground, panting. She looked up at me and said, "I'm not going anywhere with you."

"You don't have a choice," I told her.

"Hello, pretty boys," the gorgon purred. "Have you come to play with me?"

"Play has so many different interpretations," Phelan said, spinning a sword in his hand.

"Stay there while I finish this," I told Amphitrite.

"I don't take orders from you, *sea witch*."

I sighed, but turned and faced the gorgon. "Hey, mouse breath," I taunted.

She spun, hissing at me.

"I've changed my mind. I don't like the idea of them staying with you. So, you're going to let us all go, or I will kill you."

"What if we want to stay?" Wolfram asked, moving closer to the gorgon.

I narrowed my eyes at him. "Let me handle this."

"There's nothing to handle. We're going to stay here, and you can leave and take the queen home," Phelan said and moved closer to the gorgon also.

They were out of their league. She would turn them to stone before they could attack her.

"Leave, sea witch," the gorgon hissed.

I shook my head, gathering my magic in preparation.

The gorgon hissed, showing me her fangs, and launched herself at me.

I struck her in the chest, making her stagger, and stop her attack.

Her eyes turned red, and I barely had time to put up a shield to block her petrification.

The guys leapt forward, swinging swords with a shield in front of them.

She spun, knocked Phelan and Wolfram out of the air with her tail, and turned her stare on Conall, who froze in place.

"Conall!" I screamed, running towards him.

She slammed her tail into me, sending me flying towards the cliff I hadn't seen until then.

I yelped and scrambled for purchase to keep from sliding off.

Marrok grabbed me by the wrist and hauled me up. "Sorry for touching your wrist."

I chuckled. "This time, it's fine."

Wolfram and Phelan were fighting the gorgon, but they weren't able to hurt her, since her scales were so thick.

She was moving closer to Conall, and that worried me.

I ran for him, but she wrapped her tail around his petrified body, and hissed. "Everyone stop moving, or I smash him."

We all froze.

"Don't you dare hurt him," I growled at her.

"You're hiding," she said. "Why?"

"None of your business," I snapped. "Just set him down, gently, and unpetrify him."

"They don't know who you are, do they?" Amphitrite asked. She sat in the same spot I'd left her in.

"Shut up, sea queen," I snapped. "Gorgon, unless you do as I say, you're going to end up dead."

"No, I think you better do as I say, or this boy dies," she said, smirking. "It's been a long time since I've had some fun. Let's play a game."

"No," I growled.

"Let him go," Wolfram growled.

"Quiet, boy. The women are talking," the gorgon snapped.

"Why did you come?" Amphitrite asked. "I know Poseidon

43

would never have asked you to help him, even as insane as he is being right now."

"They asked me for help," I snapped at Amphitrite before facing the gorgon again. "Now, let him go and release your spell, or I'm going to skin you," I growled at the gorgon.

"Tell them who you really are, and I will let him go," the gorgon said.

"No, you won't," I said.

"Swear on my scales," she said.

I started to gather my power again, but she squeezed her tail tighter around Conall, making his stone body groan.

"Stop!" I ordered her.

Phelan started to move forward, but she flung her hand out, hitting him with a paralysis spell.

"If you interfere in my game, I will turn you all to stone," the gorgon threatened.

"I'm not playing your game," I said. I could sense water in an underground cave. If I could summon it here, I could use it to my advantage.

"Tell me your name," she said.

"Uschi," I answered.

"Your true name," she snapped, tightening her grip on Conall.

"Sea witch, just tell her," Wolfram snapped.

I flinched at the title from his lips. Apparently, I had lost all trust from them.

"My name is—"

Suddenly, Amphitrite leapt onto the gorgon and stabbed her in the back with a jagged stone.

The gorgon dropped Conall, but thankfully he didn't shatter. She tried to grab Amphitrite, but couldn't reach her.

I snatched the small bag from Marrok's sack, charged the

gorgon, and sliced one of her snakes from her head. I put it in the sack, tied it closed, and tossed it back to Marrok.

The gorgon screamed.

Wolfram stabbed his sword into the gorgon's armpit.

She screamed, and then fell to the ground, dead.

Amphitrite stood, having clung to the gorgon as she fell. "Finally."

I rushed to Conall's side, waiting as the petrification wore off. "Easy," I warned him as he sat up, gasping for air.

"That was awful," he said and shuddered.

"Amphitrite, we were sent by your husband. Please, return with us," Wolfram said and bowed to her.

"I'm not going anywhere with, Ur—" Amphitrite started to say.

I snatched her voice, putting it in my shell. "That's enough. You're going with them, and they made a deal for me to go as well. If I have to knock you out, I will."

She made a vulgar gesture, and turned, heading out of the cave.

I started to follow after her, but Wolfram stepped into my path. "If you try to double cross us—"

I bristled at the coldness in his tone and the threat. I'd just saved their asses.

"Wolfram, back down. She saved Conall," Marrok said.

"No, Amphitrite did," Phelan countered.

I stepped around Wolfram, dropped my disguise, and walked quickly out of the cave. "Don't worry, Wolfie. I'll be gone from your life soon enough."

No one spoke as we returned to the row boat. The guys dragged it into the water, and we all climbed in. I sat as far from Amphitrite as I could, sitting on a seat this time.

The guys all rowed, heading back to our boat in silence as well.

I hated this silence, but I refused to be the one to break it.

At the ship, the guys helped Amphitrite up, and she smiled seductively at them.

I bristled, but held in my anger. I had no right to it.

"Come on, Uschi," Conall said, holding out his hand over the side of the ship.

I grabbed his hand, and he hauled me up. Once on the deck, I hurried below deck, finding a spot in the storage that was empty and available for me to sit.

"Hoist the anchor!" Wolfram called.

The ship started moving, and I closed my eyes. Soon enough, I could return to my cave and forget all about this trip and these stupid boys.

CHAPTER SIX

"Uschi!" Conall yelled. "Where are you?"

"Here," I called back, rubbing my eyes as I woke fully.

Conall came into view, scowling at me. "What are you doing down here?"

"Waiting for us to reach Poseidon's," I said.

He set a tray of food on my lap. "You don't need to hide down here."

"It's better this way," I said. "Amphitrite and I don't get along."

"If you gave her back her voice, things might be better," he said with a laugh.

"Trust me, it's better this way," I mumbled and picked up one of the pieces of food, not even caring what it was.

"Why won't you tell us who you are?" he asked. "Do you really think we'll suddenly hate you just because of who you were before?"

I knew they would.

"You'll find out when we get to Poseidon's. Then, we'll see if I can say I told you so or not," I whispered.

"You saved me, again," he whispered.

47

"Amphitrite saved you," I said.

"She helped, but you're the one who distracted her long enough for them to kill her," he countered.

"She also offered us to the gorgon," Phelan said from behind Conall.

I groaned. "I did not! She asked me if I would trade you for the sea queen, and I said you weren't for sale and weren't mine."

"We aren't," Phelan said.

I glared at him. "Then she asked if she could keep you since I didn't have a claim to you. I told her to do what she wanted, but I would never have let her keep you. I planned to get Amphitrite to safety and then rescue you idiots." I stood and said, "If it weren't for me, you all would be stone right now."

"She's right," Wolfram said.

I peeked around Phelan, finding him and Marrok in the cargo area, too.

"Sure, everyone come invade my hiding spot. No problem," I grumbled.

"We could have defeated her," Phelan argued.

"We were almost turned to stone," Wolfram said. "Uschi saved us."

Hearing him say my name was both pleasant and painful at the same time.

"Great, now that we have that established, can you all buzz off and leave me alone?" I asked.

"Tell us who you are," Wolfram said. "Please."

"I can't," I whispered. "Not until we get to Poseidon."

"Do you think we'll try to kill you and claim your bounty?" he asked.

I wasn't sure anymore.

"I don't know. I just know that I don't want to have to fight you," I said softly. "We should reach Poseidon's soon. Then, I'll let you see the real me. And then, we can go our separate ways."

Tears stung my eyes, and I quickly blinked them away. I couldn't remember the last time I cried.

Wolfram's hand slid along my jaw, and tilted my face up to look at him. He searched my eyes, and then pressed his lips to mine.

I pressed into him, deepening the kiss, savoring it and committing it to memory.

He pulled back and whispered, "Thank you, for saving my brothers."

I licked my lips, and he tracked the movement with his eyes. "You're welcome," I whispered back.

"She's bewitched you, hasn't she?" Phelan asked. "All three of you."

I scoffed, bitterly. "You don't have to be a jerk all the time. I don't have the ability to bewitch anyone."

"I don't believe you," he snapped.

"I don't care what you believe," I snapped back, stepping into his space. "I'm a witch, but I don't make anyone fall in love. That's beyond my capabilities. Besides, I would never do that to anyone."

"I'll never trust you," he said. "No matter how much you bewitch the others."

I wanted to punch him, but I kept my fists at my side, and pushed past him, climbing the stairs and going to the figurehead to sit.

A day later, we arrived where we would have to dive down to go to Poseidon's.

I waited for the brothers and Amphitrite. "Ready?" I asked them.

"Ready," Wolfram said and picked up Amphitrite.

We all leapt into the water, and I held onto Conall as he swam in his seal form.

Amphitrite looked at me with a scowl.

I knew she was wondering why I didn't release my tentacles. I turned away from her, looking at Marrok. He did a spin when he saw me looking. I chuckled.

The palace came into view, and the guards let us pass when they saw Amphitrite.

We swam to the throne room where Poseidon sat. When he saw us, he stood.

Wolfram shifted forms, set Amphitrite down, and bowed. "We have returned your queen."

"My queen, are you well?"

Amphitrite opened her mouth and then pointed at her throat.

Poseidon reached out to take Amphitrite, but I swam into his path.

He glared down at me. "What is this?"

I smiled, smugly, and shifted into my true form, tentacles and all. I moaned when I was finished. "Oh, it feels good to be in my original form again. Hello, Poseidon. Did you miss me?"

"Ursula, what are you doing here?" he snapped, reaching for his trident.

I held up the shell. "No, no, Sea God. You leave that trident where it is."

"What do you want?" he snapped.

"First, lift their curse," I said.

He waved his hand and the guys groaned and then smiled.

"Done," Poseidon spat.

"Second, I want you to tell everyone that I was the one who rescued your queen. I want you to fix the tarnish that was done to my name," I said.

"What?"

"You heard me."

Amphitrite stepped up next to me and nodded at Poseidon.

He sighed and said through gritted teeth, "Fine."

I turned to Amphitrite, took her voice out of the shell, and returned it to her. "I'm sorry about that," I said softly.

She gasped in and then said, "Thank you."

"Anything else, *sea witch*," Poseidon growled.

"No, that's it," I said and turned away. "Thanks, baby."

He growled, and I felt his power crackling through the water.

I turned around. Before I could react, he pointed his trident at the selkies, and hit them with it. Their bodies convulsed, and then they minimized until they were shriveled souls.

"No!" I screamed, rushing for them.

Poseidon snatched them up, and held them near his trident. "Stop right there."

"Poseidon," Amphitrite snapped. "Stop this. She is leaving. Free those boys, and let her leave."

"She is a sea witch. She does not get to order me, a god, around," he snapped.

His eyes were wild and I detected a hint of madness there. What was wrong with Poseidon?

"Let them go. They don't have anything to do with this," I growled.

"Bow to me, and I will release them," he said, smirking.

I jerked back.

No. I had never bowed to him. I had vowed to never bow to him.

"Five. Four. Three. Two," he counted down, his power growing.

"Fine!" I screamed. "If I bow to you, you swear on your name as a god, that you will release them in their original forms without any curses?"

His power dissipated, and he nodded, his victorious smile burning my soul. "I swear on my name as a god," he said.

I swam forward, shifted my tentacles away to have legs, and dropped to my knees before him.

Poseidon bellowed with laughter and began circling me. "I never thought I would see the day that you, the mighty sea witch Ursula, would bow to me. Oh, this is a glorious day."

"Release them," I snapped.

"In a moment," he said.

"Poseidon!" Amphitrite snapped, the water swirling around her slightly.

He turned and glared at her. "What?"

"Let the boys go," she ordered. "And let her leave."

"Are you giving me an order?" he asked her.

"Do it, or I will leave, and I promise that this time you will never find me," she hissed.

"Do not threaten me," he growled and towered over her, trying to intimidate her.

She put her hands on her hips and cocked an eyebrow. "Don't try to intimidate me. I mean it. Plus, the sooner you get rid of them, the sooner we can celebrate our reunion, Posie."

Posie? Yuck.

His entire demeanor shifted at that offer. He zapped the boys back to their true forms, and waved his hand dismissively at us. "Be gone."

The boys shifted into seal forms, and swam past me, not even bothering to touch me or say goodbye.

I turned and swam away, letting my tentacles form again. Once I exited Poseidon's castle, I thought I might find the brothers waiting for me, but they were nowhere to be seen.

"You're welcome," I whispered, turning and heading towards home. It was a long swim, but I had no reason to stick around here.

Tears stung my eyes and joined the ocean's water, and I let

myself grieve for what might have been. I knew it was never going to happen, but there had been that slim chance.

I should never have let them touch me. Never again.

"I'm home," I called out as I entered my cave.

I'd expected Blackleg or one of the others to meet me outside, but hadn't seen anyone.

The main part of the cave was empty of beings, but there were random things thrown about, like someone had been inside my cave.

"Barnacle! Crustacean!" I called. "Blackleg!"

No answer.

What could have happened to them?

I swam around the rest of the cave, but found nothing and no one there. Someone had trashed my place, but it looked like it was from a struggle instead of them looking for anything.

Who? Who could have done this?

I swam back outside, and saw a note in a bottle anchored to the side of the cave. I snatched it, and swam to the surface to read the note.

Come to your true home.
If you don't, I'll kill your pets.
~Triton

I crumpled up the note and bellowed my anger. That stupid, crazy merman was going to die.

CHAPTER SEVEN

SWIMMING THROUGH THE WATERS THAT HAD ONCE BEEN my home was more painful than I thought it would be.

Many looked at me and gossiped as I passed. I didn't care. I only cared about my pets and Blackleg.

Triton would pay for his insanity.

Palace guards swam in front of me, their swords drawn and aimed at my chest.

"Halt!" one of them ordered.

I held up the note. "I've been summoned by your *king*," I hissed. "Float aside or I'll turn you into polypi."

The guards moved out of my way, but their grips tightened on their swords.

Through the palace entrance, I passed several mermaids and mermen, their brightly colored tails were beautiful, but today I did not spare them a glance.

As usual, Triton sat upon his throne with several mermaids fawning over him. He was a handsome male, had a tail colored like an oil slick that glittered in the sun, and a charming smile. He was Poseidon's son and herald.

His eyes met mine, and the madness within was startling.

How had he fallen so far in such a short amount of time?

"You received my invitation," he said, shooing the mermaids away.

"Give me my pets back," I ordered him.

"I think it's only fair that I turn them to foam, as you did my most precious daughter," he snarled.

"Your daughter made a contract with me. I did not force her. She knew the terms," I snapped.

"Lies! You tricked her! You're just an evil witch who enjoys people's suffering," he growled, rising from the throne.

He wasn't completely wrong.

"Give me my pets, or I will destroy your palace and curse you and your children," I said with a sneer.

"I think not," he said, smirking. "You see, I learned something from Poseidon."

Oh, shit. What had that double-crossing bastard done now?

"You do have a heart. But like most women, you chose poorly," he said. He snapped his fingers and Conall, Phelan, Wolfram, and Marrok swam out from behind his throne.

No. No, they wouldn't do this! They couldn't.

"Do not interfere," I warned them. "I don't want to hurt you, but I will."

Conall and Marrok looked the most unwilling, but strangely so did Wolfram.

Phelan swam right up to me. "Your reign of terror is over, sea witch."

"What reign of terror?" I asked with a scoff. "I've been living in an uninhabited lake. I haven't been causing terror anywhere. As you recall, I helped you return Amphitrite to Poseidon. How is that a reign of terror?"

"You've bewitched my brothers," he spat. "Remove your curse from them."

I shook my head. "You fool. Triton is using you and you don't even realize it."

"I understand perfectly. He is paying us, and we are putting you where you deserve," Phelan snapped.

"Where is that?" I asked.

"The dungeons," he snarled.

I gathered my power, preparing to attack Phelan, but couldn't do it. I couldn't hurt him even though he thought I was evil. Instead, I swam over him, aiming for Triton.

Wolfram and Conall caught my arms, stopping me.

"I'll kill you," I snarled at Triton.

He smiled. "Take her to the dungeons."

"I'm sorry, Uschi," Conall whispered.

"I'm sorry, too," I whispered back, and then hit him with a paralysis spell.

His body floated in the water, eyes rolled into the back of his head.

I wrapped one of my tentacles around Wolfram's arms, and twisted, making him release his hold on me.

Phelan tried to grab me, but I hit his arm with another of my tentacles, knocking him away.

I swam for Triton whose eyes were wide with fear. I created a blade of shadows and plunged it towards his chest, but Marrok swam between Triton and I.

I halted the blade and spun away from him, only to be captured by Phelan with chains around my arms.

"Don't do this," I begged Marrok. "Please."

"Take her away," Triton ordered Phelan.

Phelan struck me in the back of the head, and Marrok's sorrowful face was the last thing I saw before it all went black.

Triton stood before me, his mad eyes darting around nervously. "You've caused me great pain. So, it is only fair that I cause you great pain as well," he said.

"Die," I ordered him.

He spun his trident, and then it sliced through one of my tentacles.

I screamed and thrashed in my chains, trying to break free, but there was something wrong, something was preventing me from accessing my magic.

My black blood floated in the water.

Triton held my severed tentacle. "Did you know that you're the last Cecaelia in existence? I've been told that your pieces can fetch a decent price on the black market. I think I shall sell you off, piece by piece, until you die."

"You've gone mad," I whispered.

"You took my sanity from me," he growled.

"Then you should have protected it better. You should have been more lenient so that she did not crave the human world over yours. She craved love and attention. All she wanted was for the human to love her. It is not my fault that he did not fall for her." I swallowed.

Fear was not something I was used to. I didn't often run into situations where I had no plans for escape.

"That human lied to her and tricked her. She would have won his love, but you took her voice." His grip on my severed tentacle tightened.

"I needed payment," I said nonchalantly and shrugged a shoulder. "She had nothing else to offer."

He bellowed, and cut the tentacle he had severed earlier, even shorter.

I screamed, trying and failing again to get to my magic to hurt him.

He gripped my face so tightly that my jaw bones groaned.

"You will die, sea witch, but not before I've had my fill of torturing you as my soul is daily tortured without my youngest here."

I tried to headbutt him, but he dodged, and then punched me in the face, knocking me out.

TWO WEEKS OF TORTURE WAS MORE THAN I SHOULD HAVE had to endure. I should have died. Yet, somehow, my tentacles kept re-growing, giving Triton more time to torture me.

When he left me alone on the eighteenth day, I finally broke. I cried as I hung in the chains, my black blood surrounding me. My tears floated to join my blood, a reminder that there was no escape.

I had tried to anger Triton enough to make a mistake, but his madness was so strong that nothing I did pushed him over, since there was nowhere else to go.

The chains, I had learned, were crafted to take the magic of whoever was held by them. If only it had taken my ability to regrow tentacles as well.

Had I truly been so awful to the brothers to cause Phelan to want my death?

Hadn't I done as they'd asked and helped them find Amphitrite?

If I ever got free, I would disappear. I would never help another soul.

There was a commotion outside my cell, and then silence again.

Weird.

Blackleg walked into my cell, searching, and then his hollow sockets landed on me.

"Blackleg?" I asked softly. "What are you doing here?"

He rushed towards me, but when he reached for the chains, his body crumpled.

"Blackleg!" I gasped.

Were the chains taking the magic I had used to create him? That had to be it.

He shook like a dog and stood.

"Don't touch the chains," I ordered him. "They draw magic away. They could take the magic that I used to create you and you'll die...again."

Blackleg stood still, staring at me and the chains, and then he snapped his fingers and swam out of the dungeon.

Well, at least he was alive. Hopefully, that meant Barny and Crusty were alive, too. I hoped he freed them before he escaped.

I sagged in the chains, tired and done. Done with everything.

Triton returned, spinning his trident with a smile. "You've made me quite a bit of money. I even had someone try to purchase you from me."

I didn't bother speaking. My desire to make snide comments died two days before.

He grabbed two of my tentacles and sliced them off. I tried not to cry out, but the scream broke free anyway.

"I quite enjoy your screams," he purred. He put the tentacle pieces into a bag, and twirled the trident in front of me. "What else would someone buy? An arm? Your head?" He cut off another tentacle, laughing as I screamed.

"That's enough," a deep voice growled.

Triton spun around. "Who dares to give me an order?"

"Give me the witch," the voice said.

The voice sounded familiar.

"No. She is mine until I kill her," Triton said.

"You're not killing her," a second voice said.

That one sounded like Conall.

Power crackled in the water as Triton prepared to attack.

Blackleg darted past him, rushing to me.

"You're in so much trouble when we get home," I grumbled.

He reached for my chains again, but the instant he touched one link of chain with a single fingertip, he fell to his knees.

"Don't!" I ordered him. "You'll die. Again."

He stood, shaking his body.

Behind him Triton fought with three angry selkies. Why were they here?

Blackleg stood before me, contemplating.

"No," I snapped. "I don't know if I'll be able to bring you back if you die again. Please. Just leave me."

He reached forward with both hands, quickly flipping the lock. Then, he fell to the ground.

I drifted to the ground, and cradled his lifeless body. "No! Blackleg! No!" I didn't have enough magic to bring him back.

Triton struck Marrok, sending him flying across the room.

I set Blackleg gently back on the cell floor, and pushed off the ground, since swimming hurt my severed tentacles. I wrapped my arm around Triton's throat, and then sank my teeth into his neck.

He had taken everything from me. My home. My freedom. Turned the ones my heart desired against me. And, the only friend I'd had. My precious Blackleg.

Triton screamed and tried to dislodge me, but I held on and stole some of his magic to refuel myself. I pushed him towards Conall and his waiting sword, and then moved back to Blackleg.

Pressing my hands against Blackleg's chest, I pushed the magic power I'd stolen from Triton into him. "Live!" I ordered him. "Live!"

Blackleg's body twitched, but lay lifeless still.

"No!" I screamed and tried again, but didn't have the strength or power. Tears floated around me while I hugged

Blackleg. The stupid pirate had saved me. The brothers would have been hurt if they'd touched the chains, too, and he must have known. That must have been why he sacrificed himself. I didn't deserve him. He'd just wanted to pet sharks and find shiny things for me.

Triton screamed, and I turned to see his head float away from his body.

Good.

Wolfram swam to me, pausing when he saw my amputated tentacles still leaking black blood. "Uschi," he whispered.

I picked up Blackleg, and used my five remaining tentacles to swim out of the cell. "Piss off," I snapped.

"We're sorry. We didn't know he was going to hurt you. He paid us—"

"Happy to know you'll do anything for money. If I pay you, will you leave me alone?" I barked.

Tears floated behind me as I hugged Blackleg.

He'd saved me. I had to find a way to save him, too. He was never supposed to be brought into my issues. Triton had crossed a line bringing Blackleg into it. If he wasn't already dead, I would tear him apart limb by limb.

Conall swam closer to me, fending off a guard who tried to attack us. "We shouldn't have listened to Phelan. We didn't like doing it, but—"

"But you did. I saved you from Poseidon and you repaid me by selling me to Triton who tortured me for nineteen days. He cut off my tentacles each day and sold them to people." My breath hitched. "And now Blackleg is dead."

Crusty and Barny swam towards me beside Marrok. The dogfish zipped around me, looking healthy and whole.

I swam out of the palace, and the guys followed.

"We're sorry," Marrok said.

He reached out as if to take Blackleg.

Darkness spread out from me, and I knew my eyes were glowing as I yelled, "Don't touch him!"

The brothers halted, their eyes wide.

I glared at the brothers. "Piss off! I don't want anything to do with you disloyal, cruel, jerks! This is why I don't associate with people. All they do is stomp on your heart and destroy everything you've ever loved. Just leave me alone."

They stilled, emotions flickering across their faces.

Without another word, I returned to my home in the Dead Sea.

WETTER IS BETTER

CHAPTER EIGHT

Blackleg's crew tried to take his body from me, but I forced them out of my cave, refusing to allow them.

Crusty and Barny stayed close to me as I recovered. It took many potions and several days before I even felt halfway normal.

My heart, however, had not recovered.

I tried to put the brothers out of my mind, but they had come back for me.

Had Blackleg found them and brought them to rescue me?

On my table lay a myriad of different potions. I'd been trying a new spell that used a potion along with the spell. So far it wasn't working well.

I grabbed a dead, decaying fish from the basket beside my table, and placed it in the center of the rune circle.

"Live!" I screamed as I poured the potion onto the fish and used my spell.

The fish flopped around a bit, and then stilled.

I screamed my frustration, grabbing handfuls of my hair. Why couldn't I get this to work? I could bring the fish back with my normal spell, but that wasn't enough. I needed a better spell.

I grabbed the bag that had the gorgon snake in it, packed a few other things, and then headed out of the cave. I looked at Blackleg's first mate and said, "You are not to touch Blackleg. Protect my cave. I'm going to try to get some supplies to resurrect him. Do you understand?"

He bobbed his head.

"If his body isn't exactly where I left it when I come back, there will be hell to pay," I threatened.

He bobbed his head again and sat in front of the cave entrance.

I just had to hope that he listened to me.

With no other option, I swam off, headed to Hammerhead to buy supplies.

The swim through my tunnel brought back memories of the guys, which caused a jolt of pain through my chest.

Shove it down into that box where all the other emotions go.

Once at the island, the harpies didn't even hiss at me. They watched me with the weirdest expressions I couldn't decipher. The cyclops stepped aside, bowing his head.

What was going on?

I walked to Lansa and held out the bag. "One gorgon snake, as requested."

Her eyes widened and she hurried around her table to look at me. "You're alive."

I scowled. "I haven't been gone that long," I mumbled.

"We saw those boys. They said they didn't know where you were or what happened to you after Triton was killed," she explained.

I bristled. "Those *boys* will never know what I'm doing. They're disloyal scum."

She tilted her head to the side, a curious light in her eyes. "What happened?"

I waved my hand dismissively. "It's a long story." I looked at her table. "Sell any tentacles lately?"

Her hand flew to her mouth. "Those were yours? I didn't sell them, but I saw a new guy selling them."

My jaw tensed. "Triton cut them off to torture me."

"I tried to buy you from him, but no matter how much I offered, he refused," Hammerhead said from behind me.

I turned and smiled. "I appreciate your attempt to save me."

"I only wish I'd found those boys sooner, so I could have sent them to rescue you before you were tortured," he said.

"What?" I asked, blindsided.

"Didn't they tell you? They came here for some supplies, and I told them about your tentacles being sold. They bickered amongst themselves, and then one of the brothers got knocked out by another, and the remaining three left. They said they were going to save you," Hammerhead said.

"I wouldn't have needed saving if they hadn't worked for Triton to begin with," I snapped.

Hammerhead scowled. "They're the reason he captured you?"

"My stupidity is the reason I was captured," I said. "They were just part of my stupidity."

"We apologized," Wolfram said.

I spun and grabbed him by his throat.

"Uschi," Hammerhead snapped. "You know the rules."

I released him reluctantly.

"I need supplies," I told Hammerhead, turning my back on the guys, and handed him my list. "Once I get these I can leave."

"Please, let us talk to you," Conall begged.

"Are you performing a death ritual?" Hammerhead asked.

"No," I answered. "Do you have my supplies, or do I need to go elsewhere?"

He scowled at me. "I've got them. I'll be back."

I walked to his table and sat behind it, examining my nails.

I was well aware that they had followed me, but I refused to acknowledge them. Just knowing they were there caused an immeasurable amount of pain in my chest.

"We are sorry. We didn't know Triton would hurt you," Marrok said.

I ignored them.

"You have every right to be angry with us. We betrayed you," Conall said.

Hello, Captain Obvious. Welcome to the island.

"Please, give us another chance," Wolfram whispered.

"Another chance at what?" I asked, looking up at them. I was more shocked to find Phelan there than to find them all bowing to me.

"Another chance with you," Wolfram said.

I glared at Phelan. "You don't want a chance with me. I'm just an evil witch who seduced you."

Phelan flinched. "I don't have any excuse for my behavior, except fear."

"Fear?" I asked, arching a brow.

"I don't usually fall for women. There's never been a woman that we've all agreed on before for more than sex. Never been one we've wanted to share a relationship with before," Phelan said. "I was certain it had to be a spell. It couldn't be real."

"What can we do to earn a second chance?" Marrok asked.

"Why should I give you a chance at all? How can I trust you when you'll likely just sell me to the highest bidder? Will you chain me up and sell my parts like Triton? For all I know, you're doing this because Poseidon paid you to. To try to humiliate me."

"Here are your supplies," Hammerhead said, stopping when he spotted the boys on their knees before me.

I stood, handed him my money, and took the supplies. "Thanks, Hammerhead. I owe you a favor." I stood on my toes and kissed his cheek.

One of the boys growled, but I didn't bother looking. I kept my eyes focused ahead of me, and proudly walked out the cave while my heart broke all over again.

"Live!" I screamed, using all of my power and every ounce of my strength to resurrect Blackleg.

Blackleg's body shuddered and then he jolted upright.

Tears sprang to my eyes and I hugged him. "Blackleg."

He pushed me back and looked around the room.

"What?" I asked.

He climbed down from the table, and searched the cave, coming back to me with a scowl.

"Who are you looking for? Your crew is outside. Crusty and Barny are right there." I gestured at the dogfish floating nearby.

He tried to mime what he wanted to say, but I didn't get it.

"Look," I said. I took his glove off, and showed him his hand. "Flesh."

Blackleg looked at his new hand, mouth agape, and then he threw his arms around me and hugged me.

"Thank you for rescuing me," I whispered.

He shook his head and then made a swimming motion and then a clapping motion.

"Seals?" I guessed.

He nodded emphatically, and spread his arms out, indicating the cave.

"No, they're not here. Hopefully, I won't ever see them again," I said and turned towards the cave. "Come on, I have another surprise for you."

He floated after me, staring at his hands.

We came out of the cave, and I whistled.

A moment later, a large, undead shark with a missing eye swam over to us.

Blackleg's eye sockets widened, and he tentatively reached out a hand.

The shark bumped his nose against Blackleg's hand, and then swam closer, letting Blackleg pet him.

If he'd had eyes, or tear ducts, he might have cried.

Why didn't he have eyes? He'd gotten his flesh back, but not his tongue or eyes.

He hugged me again, and then returned to pet his shark.

"He's protected against the waters here," I explained. "But you're going to have to take him to get food every day."

He nodded, hugged his shark, and then the two of them swam away from the cave.

The joy I'd felt had given me a jolt of adrenaline, but it was gone now. I floated back into my cave and then collapsed.

Joyful tears flowed around me. I'd brought him back. And, I'd made him even happier.

Blackleg deserved more than that, but it was all I could give him. He seemed happy, though, so I supposed that was good enough.

My eyes fluttered closed, and I fell into a deep sleep.

Blackleg stood over me, a sword in one of his left hand, and his pet shark on his other side.

"What is going on?" I asked as I sat up.

Blackleg took a step forward so he wasn't standing over my body anymore, but didn't alter his stance.

I couldn't see around him.

"I've come to hire you," Hammerhead said.

I swam around Blackleg, staring at Hammerhead standing in my cave. "How are you alive?"

He smirked. "Magic, of course."

"How did you know where I lived?"

He gave me a reproachful look. "You forget who I am."

"Blackleg, how long was I asleep?"

Blackleg tapped my shoulder three times.

Three days.

"Please, I need to hire you," Hammerhead said, drawing my attention back to him.

"For what?" I asked. Hammerhead had plenty of people he could hire.

"I'll pay you whatever you want. Name your price."

"What is the job?" I asked, feeling like he was dodging the question.

"Four of my customers were kidnapped. I need you to get them back," he said.

"Kidnapped by who? For what purpose?"

Hammerhead scowled. "By the new King of the North Sea. He intends to execute them."

New King? Triton had a replacement already?

"Who took the throne?" I asked.

"Tam," he answered.

I smirked, but my thoughts were all about blood and death. "That's why you are hiring me. You know I have a bone to pick with Tam."

"I am hiring you because I think you are the only one capable of defeating Tam and saving my customers," he replied. "Plus, this has to do with you."

"Me?"

"His father is dead. Tam is doing this to get back at you," he said.

"Oh, right." I thought about that a moment and then my brows furrowed. "Your kidnapped customers wouldn't happen to be a group of selkie brothers, would they?"

"Are you going to take the job or not?" Hammerhead asked, folding his arms across his chest.

The boys had been kidnapped. Tam would likely execute them publicly for murdering his father. He would make it a grand spectacle and invite all of the merfolk and any others in his ocean to attend.

I hated Tam. Almost as much as his father. I would enjoy killing him, but to do it to save the brothers was not my idea of fun.

"They aren't my problem," I said, turning away.

"They killed him to protect you," he said.

"They wouldn't have had to protect me if they hadn't sold me to him to begin with," I snapped.

"They made a mistake. They apologized. Even the brother who is a stubborn idiot realized he was wrong. They care about you. You can't just leave them to die."

"They were going to leave me to die."

"They didn't. They came back for you."

"Only because Blackleg went and got them."

Hammerhead shook his head. "They were already on their way back for you. Blackleg met them halfway."

"Why should I bother with them? They don't know the first thing about loyalty. They'd probably just sell me out to Tam for their own freedom." I faced the wall of my cave and gnawed on my lip. As much as I wanted to leave the boys in danger, I couldn't. I knew it. Hammerhead likely knew it. That was no doubt why he had come to me.

"They're young. They were abandoned by their mothers and don't know the first thing about being demigods. You can help them. You can teach them."

"They aren't kids," I said, turning to face him. "They're adults. They are fully aware of the beds they're making and just don't want to lie in them."

"You're not going to leave those boys to die. If you do, you'll be the monster Triton always said you were. You'll be proving him right. Tam needs to die."

"Then go kill him yourself. I'm done with the merfolk and selkies," I snapped.

Hammerhead sighed and let his head drop forward. "I always knew you held grudges, but I hadn't thought about what a broken heart would do to you. Please, Uschi, Ursula, please go save them." He tossed a bag of coins on the table near the entrance of the cave. "That's a down payment. Bring those boys back to me on the island, and I'll give you the rest."

Before I could argue, he swam out of my cave.

Kill Tam and rescue the boys? Or leave them to their fate?

I wasn't a hero. I was a witch. Most thought of me as chaotic evil, but I was chaotic neutral.

Saving those boys would provide me with a large chunk of coin, but it would mean facing them again. And, they would probably think I cared for them.

"What should I do?" I asked out loud.

Blackleg swam to my room, and returned with a bag that was packed with supplies. He held it out to me.

"You think I should save them?"

Blackleg nodded.

"Fine, but this doesn't mean I like them or forgive them," I snapped and put the pack on.

He smiled, and set his hand on his shark's side.

"Don't gloat. It's unbecoming for a pirate captain," I snapped and swam out of the cave.

CHAPTER NINE

I ate as much as I could on the trip to the castle. My body had been malnourished and overused from all the magic I'd been using to perfect my spell for Blackleg, and then sleeping for three days.

If I was going to face Tam, I needed to be at full strength.

The last time I had seen Tam, I'd wrapped him up in seaweed, and sent Barny and Crusty to return him to his father. Tam had insulted me and thought I would let it pass just because his dad was the king.

Tam had done many awful things to those living in the North Sea, using his father's position as a reason people could not hurt him. His father had coddled the little turd and never reprimanded him for anything that he did.

I was looking forward to paying him back for all of the things he had done to others.

The castle came into view, and it was obvious from the guards, that things were not going well.

I approached the guards cautiously, prepared to attack.

They watched me but didn't try to stop me.

"Okay, then," I whispered as I swam inside.

The throne room had been rearranged. Tam sat upon the throne, his dark hair billowing out around him, and his tail shimmering more than usual. On either side of him were wooden stands, which the brothers hung from. Their eyes were closed, faces and bodies bloody, swollen, and discolored.

Tam smiled when he saw me, his eyes sparkling with mirth. "Ursula, you came."

"I heard you were being an epic prick again, so I decided it was time to stop you. Your entire family needs to be wiped out." I stopped a bit away from him, trying to avoid looking at the guys.

"You dare disrespect the king?" he asked. He stood and grabbed the trident from the stand he had it set in.

"Release these selkies, and let us finish our fight," I ordered him.

"These cretins murdered my father. They are to be executed," Tam said. He spun the trident, and then stabbed Phelan in the side. Phelan cried out, and his blood floated around the trident.

"Each of these disloyal, murderous cretins is ten times the man you will ever be," I snapped.

"You care for them? I had been told this, but thought it had to be false. The evil sea witch has feelings?"

"The evil sea witch is here to end the tyranny and destruction you will wreak on the ocean," I growled. With a deep breath, I gathered some of my magic, putting a small shield around myself.

Tam smirked, spun the trident, and moved to the other side of his throne, stabbing Wolfram.

Without hesitation, I hit Tam with a sea urchin spine, the spine was coated in a paralysis toxin.

It struck his shoulder, and he screamed out in pain, and then his arm went limp. He glared at me. "What sorcery is this?"

I moved the shield from myself to the boys, so he wouldn't be able to hurt them anymore. "Fight me, you coward-ass carp."

Tam roared, his eyes full of fury and little thought, and charged me. He swung his trident carelessly, and I dodged it easily.

"What's it like ruling people who think you're nothing more than an algae eating snail?" I wrapped a tentacle around his paralyzed arm, squeezing tightly, and then used it to swing him in a circle before throwing him into the wall.

He pushed off the wall and screamed wordlessly at me. He tried to stab me with the trident, but I deflected it with one of my tentacles and slapped him across the face with another tentacle.

"Are there any mermaids who want to sleep with you of their own free will? Even Triton had mermaids fawning over him, but it seems that gene didn't pass down to you."

My slap had left red circles on his cheek, which made me smile.

"What's it like never being loved?" he asked, catching my shoulder with a punch. "What's it like knowing everyone thinks you're an evil witch who can only gain love with spells and hypnosis." He stabbed one of my tentacles with the trident and sent a current of electricity through me.

I cried out, but quickly kicked him in the stomach, and removed the trident from my tentacle. The idiot hadn't held onto the trident, and I now had it.

I smiled victoriously. "It's over, snail bait." I closed my eyes, raised the trident over my head, and channeled all of my power into it. My body expanded, growing three times its normal size. I laughed maniacally, the sound very evil witch sounding, and I loved it.

He tried to attack me, but since he was so much smaller, I could easily bat him aside with my tentacles. I hit him again and again, and then slammed him to the ground, pressing down hard as I pinned him to the ocean floor.

He cried out, and the sound caused shivers of delight to race up my spine. I wrapped one of my tentacles around his throat and lifted him.

He gasped for air, my grip keeping his gills closed, and clawed at my tentacles.

He stabbed the tentacle around his throat with a small dagger, and I was forced to release him. I tucked the injured tentacle inside of the others, to protect it.

He charged me, trying to get the trident, but I swung it into his side, sending him spinning. Carefully aiming, I shot the chains off of the guys, and then aimed the trident at Tam's chest.

"Beg," I ordered.

"I don't beg women," he said.

"No, you just force them to screw you with no regard for how they feel. No longer. You will never rape another mermaid. You will never hurt another soul. I banish you from this world."

"You can't kill me! I'm the king," he spat, his eyes wild and reminiscent of his father.

Was it the trident? Did it cause them to go insane?

I propelled myself forward, and stabbed the trident into Tam's chest, thrusting hard enough that the three tips poked out of his back.

He coughed blood, and his eyes widened.

"No one is invincible," I whispered.

"Not even you," he whispered and stabbed something into my chest.

I gasped in pain and yanked the trident free from his body. He dropped to the ocean floor, dead.

Glancing down, I cursed, but the numbness spreading through me was sign enough. He'd stabbed me with the sea urchin needle. The toxin reached my heart, and it seized up in response.

I sank down, and closed my eyes.

It was fine. I'd saved the guys. Blackleg was healed and had a shark. And, I'd ended the tyranny of this family. There was nothing else that I needed to do.

"Uschi," Wolfram called weakly.

The darkness surrounded me and I welcomed it. The darkness was my friend.

"You're so damn troublesome," Lansa said.

My body felt like it was on fire. "I need the darkness," I whispered, squeezing my eyes closed tightly.

"You need to wake up," Hammerhead said.

"Am I in a cave?" I asked. "One full of vendors?"

"Possibly," Hammerhead said, the humor evident in his tone.

"Why am I not dead?" I asked.

"You almost were. The boys had to take turns carrying you here. They're still in poor shape, but much more lively than you," Lansa said.

"I don't want to open my eyes," I said. "If I keep them closed, I can keep thinking I'm still dead. Being dead was good. It was quiet and there were no problems."

"You killed Tam," Hammerhead said.

"Yes."

"You're still holding the trident," Lansa said. "The guys couldn't get you to let go."

I bolted upright and tossed the trident away from myself. "No!"

Hammerhead and Lansa stared with wide eyes.

"It's cursed," I told them. "It makes the one wielding it go mad."

"No, two mad men were owners of it," Hammerhead said. Maybe.

"Just, don't let anyone touch it," I mumbled and laid back down, groaning. Why did not dying have to hurt so much?

"Uschi?" Phelan called.

"I'm dead," I said. "Leave me alone."

"Dead people don't talk," Phelan argued.

"Only if fish ate their tongues first," I mumbled.

"What?" Lansa asked.

"She has an undead pirate. He can't talk because fish ate his tongue before she resurrected him," Hammerhead explained.

"You brought something back to life?" Lansa gasped.

"Twice, technically," Phelan said.

"Uschi, what is wrong with you?" Lansa snapped. "You can't bring things back from the dead."

"Whoops," I said with a smirk.

"Please tell me it's just the one," Lansa said and sighed. She sounded like a disappointed mother.

"Six," Wolfram answered.

"Seven," I corrected.

"Seven?" Wolfram asked. "What else did you bring back to life?"

"A shark," Hammerhead said.

"Why are we talking about me? I'm dead. Leave me in peace."

I could hear the eyes rolling.

"You're not dead," Phelan said and took my hand.

I opened my eyes, staring at our joined hands.

"You saved us, again." Phelan raised my hand and kissed my knuckles. "We're in your debt."

I pulled my hand away and sat up. "I don't keep debts. Just leave me alone and we'll be equal."

"Lansa, will you help me over here?" Hammerhead asked, pulling her out of the room we were in, and leaving me alone with the brothers.

"Traitor!" I yelled.

I flexed my muscles and looked down at my tentacles. This was the first time I'd been in the cave without legs.

Wolfram traced one of my tentacles with his fingertip, making me shudder. "I never thought I'd say that I like tentacles, but I do."

"What do you want?" I asked and transformed. I wasn't embarrassed of my tentacles, but in the black market I always had legs.

"We're sorry," Phelan said. "Please, forgive us." He walked around me, and knelt at my feet. "I'm sorry. I'm an idiot."

"You can say that again," I scoffed.

"I'm a huge idiot. I understand you not liking me, but don't punish my brothers." He met my eyes, and the pleading in them tore at my heart.

"What happens if I forgive you jerks?" I asked, folding my arms over my chest.

"We start taking you out on dates," Conall said, coming around so I could see him.

"Dates?" I had never been on a date before.

"Fun things like the night we met in the bar," Marrok said. He stopped on my right side, his body so close that I could feel his heat.

"All of you?" I asked.

They all nodded.

"You've got your mojo back. You could go find a hundred women each." Not that I wanted them to, but they could.

"Go on an adventure with us," Wolfram said. "You can

leave at any time."

"What kind of adventure?" I asked.

"Treasure hunting," Conall said with a wide smile.

I did love a good treasure hunt.

"Are we swimming or taking a ship?" I asked. Not that it mattered. I liked both.

"Ship most of the way," Wolfram said.

"How long will this adventure take?" I didn't want to leave Blackleg and my pets alone for too long.

"A month, or so," Wolfram said. "Why? You have a hot date?"

I smirked. "Maybe."

That had all of the guys scowling.

Interesting.

"I need to go home first," I said. "So, Blackleg and his crew don't think I'm dead."

"We need to gather supplies still," Marrok said. "So, that works for us."

"Meet here in two days?" Conall asked.

I shrugged and then nodded. "Sure."

"Let's go start gathering things now," Wolfram said to Marrok.

Conall nodded, kissed my cheek, and then left the room.

Wolfram kissed my cheek, as did Marrok on their way out.

Had I been a woman who blushed, I would have been burning up.

"I really am sorry," Phelan said. He and I were the last ones in the room.

"I'm going to go on this adventure with you, but you guys haven't earned back my trust yet. I was tortured for weeks because of you guys."

"Because of me," he said.

"What made you change your mind?" I asked.

"I had been trying to push you away the entire trip. Wolfram had been as well. Then he started falling for you, too. It scared me. He didn't ever fall for women. I started falling for you, shortly after, and that terrified me. What would happen if you came between us? I was just a scared, pathetic boy, and my fear cost you."

"You aren't still worried that I'll come between you?" I asked.

He smirked. "No. If anything, you've brought us closer together."

"That may change if one or more of you sleep with me." I would totally be okay with that, though.

"No, it won't," he said with such conviction that I was certain they had discussed it already.

"So, you've already discussed sleeping with me?" I asked, smirking.

He stepped forward, close enough I had to tilt my head up to look at him. "Yes. And fantasized about it. And pleasured myself thinking about it."

My mouth popped open.

He moaned. "Don't tease me, Uschi."

"I'm not—"

He leaned down and kissed me. I expected it to be demanding or fierce, but it was tender. He pulled back too soon and said, "I'm really looking forward to our trip."

I went up on my tiptoes and whispered in his ear, "If you try to screw me over this time, I'm going to kill you all."

He wrapped his arms around my waist and hugged me, whispering into my ear, "I am aware, and I will fully support your decision if that does happen."

He released me and left with a wide smile on his face.

I really didn't trust them fully, but I was not going to pass up this opportunity.

CHAPTER TEN

Blackleg was ecstatic about me going on the trip. He packed my bag for me, and shoved me out of the cave the following day.

The harpies no longer hissed at me when I swam up to the island, and the cyclops stepped to the side for me.

I wasn't sure how to react to no longer being viewed as evil, at least by these people.

The guys stood together in front of Hammerhead's table.

I stopped, giving myself some time to stare at the men I was going to be seducing.

I'd decided that this was likely to be a short-lived romance, so I was going to have as much fun as I could. Part of that fun included trying to seduce as many of the brothers as possible. Even multiple at the same time, if luck was on my side.

"Uschi," Conall said as he turned and spotted me.

The others turned as well, their eyes lighting up as they smiled.

I waved, felt like a moron, and dropped my hand quickly. "Hey."

"Ready?" Marrok asked.

I nodded and gripped my pack straps.

"Uschi," Lansa called.

I turned towards her voice and headed to her table, where she stood, scowling.

"What's up?" I asked.

"Here," she whispered and held out a small bag. I took it, and started to open it, but she placed her hand on top of mine. "No. Don't show them."

"What is it?" I asked.

"I don't know much about Cecaelia, but I'm certain you are able to get pregnant. This will keep you from getting pregnant during your adventure," she said, smirking.

I laughed and then hugged her. "You're the best. Thank you." I didn't feel like bursting her bubble by telling her I was infertile.

"Have fun and bring me back the juicy details," she said and laughed.

I winked. "You got it."

The guys all had an arched brow when I made it to them, but I just smiled sweetly.

"Do we have a ship?" I asked. I hadn't seen one when I'd entered, but there were docks on other parts of the island.

"On the north side," Wolfram said.

"Uschi," Hammerhead called.

I turned. "Yeah?"

"Do me a favor?" he asked.

I put a hand on my hip. "What?"

"Bring me back some sea water from the Pacific Ocean," Hammerhead said and held out a jar. "I'll pay you well for it."

"Just some water?" I asked, skeptical.

He nodded.

"I'll try," I said and put the jar and the bag from Lansa into my pack.

"Ready now?" Phelan asked.

I nodded.

They led the way, and I waved to Hammerhead and Lansa as I walked after the guys.

The guys chattered quietly amongst themselves, and I ignored most of it.

Marrok fell back to walk beside me. "We're all really excited," he said.

I nodded and smiled. "I am, too. It's been a long time since I've done a treasure hunt."

"Have you ever been to the Pacific Ocean?" he asked.

I nodded. "Once, but I didn't stay for very long. The water isn't very clear, and I kept getting attacked by weird creatures."

"Creatures?" he asked.

I nodded. "They looked like large sharks, but were much more intelligent. I'm not sure what they were."

"How long ago was that?" he asked.

"Just a couple of years ago," I said. "Right after the incident with the mermaid."

"Why'd you go to the Pacific?"

I sighed. "I was trying to find a new place to live, since Triton kicked me out of his waters."

"I'm glad he's dead, but I wish we'd made him suffer a bit more."

I chuckled. "You and me both. And his kelp-brained son. I wanted to make him pay for making you guys suffer like you did, but it was better that he just died."

"You almost died as it was," he whispered.

I nudged his shoulder with mine. "We all survived. Let's leave it in the past."

We lapsed into silence, walking out of the northern entrance, and to a large ship with a pirate flag blowing in the wind.

"Nice ship," I said.

"Thanks," Wolfram said. "The crew who had been using it weren't very bright."

"No?" I asked.

"They lost it to us in a game of cards," Wolfram said and then he and his brothers laughed.

"Rigged cards?" I asked.

"We never cheat," Wolfram said, smirking.

"Not you boys, of course not," I said and chuckled.

"We actually didn't cheat them. They were just so drunk that they kept giving away their hands, or letting the cards drop and showing the hand to us," Phelan said. "I don't think I've ever seen such drunk pirates before."

"That's pretty common for them," I said. "I've won my fair share of items from them that way."

We boarded the ship, and I walked into the captain's quarters, and lay on the bed.

Wolfram entered with a smirk. "Claiming your room?"

"Well, either you four would have to fight over this room, flip a coin, or something, or I could just take it. Really, it's only fair of you to offer it to me since you invited me on this journey," I said.

He sat beside me and asked, "Do any of us get to share this cabin with you?"

I sat up, pressing our chests together, and asked, "Are you saying you want to share this cabin with me, Wolfram? There are prices to pay for sharing a cabin with me."

"Prices?" he asked, leaning closer, our mouths a breath apart. "What price are you speaking of?"

I licked my lips, which caused me to lick his lips as well. "Steep prices," I whispered.

His mouth crashed into mine, desire surging within us both and turning a simple kiss into a torrent of lips and tongues.

"We ready to go?" Conall asked from the doorway.

Wolfram pulled back, licking his lips while staring into my eyes. "Yes, we're definitely ready to go."

He left the room, and I fell onto my back with a happy smile on my face.

Yes, we were definitely ready to go.

The boys expertly sailed the ship away from the dock. I took a seat on the figurehead, wrapping a few of my tentacles around it to keep me secure. Not that it would matter if I fell in anyway.

Conall stood at the railing behind me, looking out over the ocean. "You know what we haven't done yet?" he asked.

"What?" I asked, twisting my upper body to look back at him.

"Gone swimming together," he said.

"We swam together a few times," I said.

"Not for fun though," he said and stuck his lip out in a pout.

I laughed. "We can go swimming whenever you want, selkie boy."

"I have the perfect spot planned out," he said and walked away smiling. "I can't wait."

A few hours later, my eyes began to grow heavy. I shifted my tentacles to legs, and climbed back onto the deck, headed towards my cabin.

I pushed the door open, and found all of the brothers inside, sitting around the table inside, playing cards.

"Who's sailing the ship?" I asked, eyes wide.

"It's set to go in one direction. We're fine," Marrok said.

I turned on my heel and marched up to the wheel, staring at the rope he'd used to secure it. No. There was no way I was riding on a ship that was not being steered. There were enough creatures that lived in these waters that would take advantage of an unmanned ship to cause havoc.

The brothers came out, all scowling at me.

"I'm not risking it," I told them and grabbed the wheel.

Wolfram sighed, climbed the steps, and bumped me with his hip, taking control of the wheel from me. "I've got it. You look like you're ready to fall over."

Marrok swept me up in his arms and carried me into the cabin. Then, he dumped me on the bed with a wicked grin. "Take a nap, Uschi. We're going to play cards."

I kicked the back of his knee, making his leg buckle as he walked away, and laughed when he gave me a glare.

Laying on my side, I watched the boys playing the card game. It was one I was unfamiliar with.

"What's this treasure we're searching for?" I asked around a yawn.

"A secret," Marrok said without looking at me.

I rolled my eyes.

"It's about the journey, not the destination," Phelan said.

If I rolled my eyes any harder, they'd get stuck in the back of my skull.

"How many more times can we make her roll her eyes tonight?" Conall asked.

Flipping over, I faced the wall.

"I think she's pouting," Conall whispered.

"Or resting because she's tired," I muttered with my face pressed into the pillow.

"Then take a nap," Conall said.

Try as I might, I couldn't.

With a groan, I rolled out of bed, ignored the guys and their stupid expressions, and headed up to Wolfram.

He arched a brow, but wisely said nothing.

I sat on top of the railing that was in front of the wheel, but off to the side, so I wasn't blocking Wolfram's view.

"Couldn't sleep?" he asked.

"No."

"Well, I won't complain. You're welcome to sit with me anytime that you can't sleep," he said.

I turned and smirked at him. "Thanks for the invitation."

The sun set, and the sirens started their songs.

"Their songs are actually pretty, if you aren't worried about them trying to murder you," Wolfram said.

I groaned.

"Well, it's true," he said.

I sighed. "I agree. I just don't like admitting it."

The other guys came out of the cabin and peered over the edges of the ship.

I gripped the railing, the urge to call out to them, or tear the sirens apart, was so strong I almost couldn't control myself.

"They're not going to be lured in," Wolfram said. I could hear his barely contained laughter.

"If those were male sirens, and I was leaning over the edge, would you want to grab me and pull me away?" I asked.

He didn't answer, so I turned to look at him. His scowl was answer enough.

"Exactly," I said, smiling smugly.

"Sea witch," one of the sirens called.

I hopped off the railing, walked to the edge, and looked over at her. "Yes?"

A siren and two of her sisters swam beside the ship.

The siren who had spoken to me said, "We are sorry for perpetuating that piece of trash's lie about you."

My eyes widened. A siren had just apologized to me. Was the world ending? "Thank you," I said.

"But, you're still an evil sea witch," another of them said.

All three cackled.

I laughed myself and waved to them. "Have a good night! I hope you find a few sailors to murder."

"We will," all three chorused as they swam away.

CHAPTER ELEVEN

"Favorite sea mammal?" Conall asked.

"Whale," I said.

They'd been asking me questions for several hours while we all lay on the deck, absorbing the warmth of the sun. They said it was to get to know me better. I was certain it was to kill their boredom.

Either way, I was fine with their plan.

"Favorite land mammal?" Wolfram asked.

"Jaguar," I said.

"Saw that coming," Marrok said and chuckled.

"What's that supposed to mean?" I asked and tilted my head to the left to look at him.

They'd lain around so that our heads formed a circle. In the middle sat a jug of water for whoever got thirsty.

"If you were to transform into a land mammal, I'm certain it would be a jaguar," Marrok said. "It fits you."

"Because it's viewed as evil?" I asked and arched a brow.

"Because it's dark, feisty, and powerful," Marrok said and leaned over to give me a peck on the cheek.

I smirked and looked back up at the clouds passing overhead. Alright, he got points for that answer.

"Favorite marsupial?" Conall asked.

Everyone looked at him.

"What the heck is a marsupial?" Phelan asked.

"You know, like a kangaroo or koala," Conall said.

I smirked, knowing of one they probably didn't even know existed. "Opossum."

As expected, all eyes turned towards me.

"What?" Marrok asked.

I waved my hands in the air, using my magic to conjure up an image of one of the hideous little beasts that roamed North America. "This is an opossum."

"It's ugly," Conall said and frowned.

"Tasmanian Devil," Wolfram said. "That's what Uschi would be."

"Why do you keep bringing up which animal I would be?" I asked, scowling.

"It's part of the game," Phelan said.

"Favorite flower?" Marrok asked.

"Hibiscus," I said.

"That's the one on the island with volcanoes, right?" Conall asked.

I nodded.

"Rose," Phelan said. "That's Uschi."

I smiled. "Because it's pretty, but has thorns? Or because it's often used to curse people?"

"It's used to curse people?" Conall asked.

I nodded. "Yep."

"Favorite food?" Wolfram asked.

"Bread. Of any kind," I said immediately.

"Favorite sweet?" Phelan asked.

"Caramel," I said.

"You're chocolate," Marrok said.

"Because it's bitter like I am?" I asked, scowling.

Silence greeted me. I sat up and found them all doubled over, holding their stomachs and laughing silently.

"Let it out," I said and sighed.

All four boomed with laughter, and I found myself smiling. They had made me smile quite often on this trip already.

We'd been sailing for a while, and I felt like the waters looked familiar, but I wasn't positive.

"Which path are we taking to the Pacific?" I asked, getting up and walking to the side of the ship.

I could see land in the near distance, but the rocky shores didn't look familiar.

"We'll be out of this area soon enough," Wolfram growled from behind me.

"We'll be entering cold water soon, so you should be ready to bundle up," Conall said.

A sound filtered to me along the breeze, and I spun around with a wide smile. "I know where we are!"

I raced to the wheel, untied it, and spun it to change our trajectory.

The guys groaned as they slid on the deck on their backs.

"What are you doing, you crazy woman?" Marrok barked.

"Bagpipes!" I yelled joyously. "I hear bagpipes."

The guys groaned.

"So?" Phelan asked.

"I love bagpipes," I said, headed towards the closest dock.

A chorus of groans answered my statement.

"Really?" Marrok asked. "You're going to subject us to bagpipes?"

I turned and arched a brow. "Aren't you selkies from Ireland?"

They all nodded.

"So, you're used to bagpipes?"

"Doesn't mean we like them," Phelan muttered and crossed his arms over his chest.

I tensed. "Really? You don't like bagpipes?" I'd wanted to go listen to the bagpipes because I liked them, and assumed the guys would, too. I wouldn't force that on them if they hated it, though.

I sighed and turned the ship, heading away from land.

Wolfram caught one of the wheel's handles, stopping it from spinning. "If you want to land and listen, we'll go."

"I don't want you to do something you don't want, something you don't enjoy," I said, pushing at his hold.

"Uschi, let me steer," Wolfram said, stepping closer to me.

I stepped aside and let him take over.

"We haven't been here in a long time," Phelan whispered as he looked towards the dock.

"Ten years, at least," Conall agreed.

"Think Mom's still here?" Marrok asked.

"Most likely," Connall said.

"Let's try to avoid your mother," Phelan said and grimaced.

I'd forgotten that they were half-brothers, coming from the same father who was a god.

"Why were you so easily defeated by Tam?" I asked, growing suspicious now that I'd remembered they were demigods.

"He used those power sucking chains on us," Wolfram answered. "He actually had a net made of them and dropped it on us."

I grimaced. That had to have hurt.

Wolfram guided the ship to the dock, and the guys made quick work of tying it up.

Humans at the docks watched us curiously, but none stopped us or approached.

Wolfram and the others hopped off the ship onto the deck without a plank. I stood on the railing with my hands on my hips. Did they expect me to jump, too? I could, but I'd need to use my magic to help me land, and the humans wouldn't react kindly to that.

Wolfram smirked and held up his arms. "Come on, beautiful."

I sighed, but jumped without hesitation.

Wolfram caught me easily, kissed my temple, and then set me on my feet. "Let's go find you some bagpipes." He slipped his fingers between mine, and squeezed our joined hands.

I squeezed back, beaming up at him. I had never had a man hold my hand for a stroll through the town before.

Conall walked in front of us, while Phelan and Marrok walked behind us.

Women fanned themselves, men scowled, and I smiled. The humans were such prudes.

Dressed in pants and a shirt, I looked like a pirate, since most women wore pretty dresses.

While I enjoyed wearing dresses every now and then, I couldn't fathom wearing them every day.

The sound of bagpipes grew louder as we walked through the port town.

Wolfram stopped at a baker, purchased a cream stuffed pastry, and handed it to me.

I took a huge bite, groaning when the cream hit my tongue in a sweet burst. "So good," I moaned.

All of the guys turned to look at me, watching as I licked the cream that had gotten on my lips.

Wolfram kissed me deeply, sliding his tongue along mine, and pulled back with a wide smile. "It is sweet."

I almost crushed the pastry in my grip. "Tease," I said breathlessly.

Women had gasped behind us when he kissed me, but I was more worried about the flood waiting to burst from between my legs if he did that again.

"Promises for later," he whispered in my ear.

I squeezed my legs together tightly.

They resumed walking, and I followed them to the town square.

The buildings were built to allow a large circular area in the middle of the town. Though it was currently filled with people dancing, smiling, and listening to the three men playing bagpipes, they also used this area for hangings and executions.

The brothers stood around me in a protective circle, on the outskirts of the dancers to keep me from being bumped into, and listened to the music.

Phelan stood at my back and stepped up right behind me, pressing his chest to my upper back as he whispered in my ear. "Would you like to dance?"

I nodded and tilted my head back so I could look up at him. "Yes, please."

He spun me around, slid an arm around my waist, and then took my other hand. "Boys, we're going dancing."

Marrok and Wolfram stepped to the side so we could merge into the large group of dancers.

Phelan smiled down at me as we spun with the others, moving around the square, spinning around the bagpipe players.

I returned the smile, laughing when he raised his hand and I spun beneath it. He caught me, pressing us close together, and we resumed our dance.

An arm caught me around the middle, pulling me away from Phelan. I was prepared to attack, and then I realized it was Marrok.

He smirked but said nothing as we danced.

Another arm snaked out, stealing me from Marrok.

This time it was Conall.

He opened his mouth, but Wolfram snagged me away.

Conall scowled, which made me laugh.

I wasn't sure how long we danced, or how many times I danced with each of the guys, but by the time the sun set, my face hurt from smiling and laughing so much.

I leaned against Wolfram, breathing heavily. "You boys sure know how to dance."

"They ought to, since I taught them," a gravelly male voice said.

Wolfram turned, hiding me behind him. "What are you doing here?" he growled.

"You came to my sea, to my island, and didn't expect me to know?" the stranger asked. "Really?"

"We figured you were too busy to pay us any mind," Phelan said, coming to my side with clenched fists.

Marrok and Conall came to us as well, all standing around me protectively.

"Look at you four, acting so possessive of a woman. This one must be special if all four of you are acting this way," the man said.

"What do you want?" Wolfram asked.

"I came to see my sons and find out why they're visiting, since they hated it here so much," the man said.

Their dad. It had to be their dad.

I tapped Wolfram's shoulder, but he just growled.

"Wolfram," I whispered.

Wolfram sighed and stepped to the side, letting me step between him and Phelan to view the man.

Before me stood a man with every good aspect of my boys rolled into one, glorious, red-haired package. He was no doubt, a god. And, I knew him.

"Muirin," I said and smiled wide.

Muirin looked at me and his eyes widened. "Urs—"

"I go by Uschi now," I said and stepped forward.

He took my hands, raised one, and kissed my knuckles gently. "You're even more beautiful. How is that possible?"

I stood on tip toe and kissed his cheek. "You're even more handsome than I remembered, but you are a god."

He smiled at me and then drew me in for a hug. He pushed me back and said, "I heard what Triton did to you. I'm sorry. You know you are always welcome in my seas. I would have built you a new home. A better home."

I stepped back. "It worked out. I met some fun guys who are taking me on an adventure."

He looked over my head. "Them? You're running around with my boys?"

"I didn't know they were yours until just now," I said.

"What's going on?" Wolfram asked. "How do you know our father?"

"The adults are talking," Muirin snapped. "Quiet."

"Muirin, how could you let Poseidon curse them?" I asked with my hands on my hips and a chastising tone. "You should have beaten that idiot to a pulp for doing such a thing to your children."

"He did what?" Muirin asked, his body glowing, and eyes flaring with fire.

CHAPTER TWELVE

"Whoops," I whispered and turned to face the guys. "I think I just ratted you out to your dad."

"How do you know him?" Marrok asked. "Were you two...involved?"

I laughed so hard that I doubled over, clutching my stomach with one arm while holding onto Muirin with my other arm to keep from falling to the ground.

"It's not that funny," Muirin grumbled.

I straightened and wiped the tears from my eyes. "You four are hilarious. Of course your dad was never involved with me." I pointed at Muirin. "God." I pointed at me. "Sea witch."

"Has she always been like this?" Wolfram asked Muirin.

Muirin nodded. "Since she was a teenager."

"I'm standing right here," I said, putting my hands on my hips.

"Isn't Poseidon your ex?" Conall asked. "And isn't he a god?"

"Yes, but Greeks sleep with anything, so they don't count," I said.

"Back to the point!" Muirin snapped. "What did Poseidon do to my sons?"

"Made them, uh…" I stopped talking and looked back at the guys. "Maybe you should tell him."

"Let's go to my house," Muirin said.

"But the bagpipes," I pouted.

"They'll be here later," Muirin promised.

I walked beside Muirin, well aware of the boys fuming behind us. "They're very curious how we know each other," I whispered.

Muirin draped his arm across my shoulders and pulled me into his side. Warmth flowed from him into me, joy filling me at the touch from a god. "Let them wonder a bit longer," he whispered in my ear.

"I see where they get their flirtatiousness from," I mumbled.

Muirin tossed his head back and laughed.

A portal opened in front of us, and I looked around, worried the humans would see us.

"The humans won't see us," Muirin said. He waved me towards it. "Ladies first."

"If there's a monster again, I'll—"

"Not this time," he said and smirked.

"Again?" Wolfram asked.

"What monster?" Conall asked.

I stepped through, to avoid answering them, and looked around Muirin's palace. It looked the same as the last time I had seen it, fifteen or so years ago.

The palace was on a small island off the coast of Ireland, and made completely from marble. Fur rugs lay in the living room around the furniture, and a fire roared in the fireplace.

I sat on the fur rug before the fireplace, holding my hands out to warm them.

The guys teleported into the room, searched for me, and then took seats on the couches behind me.

Muirin sat in his high-backed seat reminiscent of a throne, and glared at his sons. "What happened?"

"We handled it," Phelan said.

"We'd rather discuss how you know Uschi," Wolfram said.

Was that jealousy in his voice? Even after I'd laughed at the notion?

"Poseidon first," Muirin snapped.

"He cursed us. We had to go find his missing wife and return her," Marrok said.

"Cursed you how?" Muirin asked.

I held up my pointer finger and then let it droop.

Muirin's power flared behind me, making me cringe.

"Why was I not involved?" he asked.

"You've not wanted to be involved before," Wolfram said. "Why would we think this time was different?"

"Because another god messed with my children. That is inexcusable," Muirin said.

"We told you, now tell us about Uschi," Conall said.

"She helped me with a matter," Muirin said vaguely.

"Uschi," Wolfram said.

"I was not involved with your father intimately," I said.

"Not because I didn't try," Muirin whispered.

"I helped him find a missing selkie," I said. "She'd been kidnapped by a group of harpies who wanted to use her to feed their hatchlings."

"They'd taken her far inland, to a place outside of my jurisdiction," Muirin added. "Ursula—"

"Uschi," the guys and I corrected him at the same time.

"Uschi, rescued her for me. She also refused to let me pay her," Muirin said.

I turned and smiled up at the scowling god. "Your sons can pay me later on your behalf."

Muirin scowled. "I'm not sure how I feel about you being with them."

The guys tensed.

"I'm not with them yet. They still have to prove themselves to me," I said.

"We hurt her, so we're trying to make up for it," Phelan said.

"What did you idiots do to her?" Muirin demanded.

"Handed me over to Triton so he could torture me," I said nonchalantly.

"We didn't know!" they all shouted.

Muirin stood, his entire body glowing, and his eyes a living flame. "You four, in my chambers, now."

"Don't be too hard on them, Muirin. They've apologized and are trying to make up for it," I said.

"They have more to tell me, but for some reason, don't want to in front of you," Muirin said. "They're going to come with me and tell me everything."

"Can I have food?" I asked.

Muirin snapped his fingers and a feast appeared on a long table behind the couch the boys sat on.

"Score!" I cheered and hurried around them to make myself a plate.

"We'll be back," Wolfram whispered in my ear and kissed my cheek.

"Don't hurt them!" I called after Muirin.

"If they need punished, they'll be punished," Muirin called. "I have a feeling they do."

"Sorry," I whispered to the guys, but they each kissed my cheek and followed after their father.

I should have felt bad for getting them in trouble, but I knew

Muirin wouldn't actually hurt them. As tough as he acted, he really was a sweetheart inside.

After piling a plate high with food, I sat on the fur rug before the fireplace and ate. The food was incredible — the most delicious food I had ever eaten.

The palace shook as Muirin roared, "What?"

I chuckled and continued eating.

I should have distrusted the guys more. I should have still been mad. I wasn't, though. It was strange because I usually harbored grudges, but for some reason, I wasn't harboring this one with them.

I was different with them in a lot of ways.

Muirin marched back into the room, the boys behind him with their heads hanging.

I turned my back to the fire, still eating from my plate.

Muirin dropped to one knee and bowed his head. The boys followed his lead.

"We, of the House of Selkies, are sorry for the grievances caused upon you by the four idiots I spawned," Muirin said.

The boys were quiet until Muirin elbowed Wolfrom in the side.

"We are sorry for the grievances caused upon you," all four said.

"We owe you a debt," Muirin said. "What price would you ask of me?"

"I don't know," I said, frowning. "I saved them twice and they betrayed me. That's not a simple, give me a pretty dress type of debt."

Muirin growled and nodded. "I agree. This debt is very large."

"Can I think about it?" I asked.

Muirin nodded. "I owe you two debts. My sons owe you one each."

I smiled. "I accept."

They stood, and the boys immediately filled up plates of food for themselves, and then sat beside me on the rug.

"Where are you headed?" Muirin asked, sitting in his chair and watching us with a strange glimmer in his eyes.

"Pacific," Wolfram answered around the food in his mouth.

"Treasure hunt," Phelan said.

Muirin's left eyebrow arched up. "Treasure hunt?"

All the guys nodded.

"What type of treasure?" Muirin asked.

I held still, waiting for them to spill about the story.

"Secret," Marrok answered.

"We're keeping it a secret from Uschi," Wolfram said and smiled at me.

"Watch out for the sea monsters," Muirin said. "They get quite big there."

"That's what I told them," I said and smiled.

"Why were you in the Pacific?" Muirin asked.

"Searching for a new home," I admitted.

He scowled. "Is there a reason my seas aren't good enough for you?"

Whoops. I'd pissed off a god. Not a good idea.

"I didn't want to invade," I said. "Or overstep my boundaries. I had assisted you before, but that didn't mean I was welcome."

Muirin sighed. "You are always welcome here, Ursula."

"Uschi," the four brothers said.

Muirin smirked. "Uschi."

I bowed my head. "Thank you."

"Where are you living now?" Muirin asked.

"The Dead Sea," Wolfram said with a scowl. "We can't even see her place or we'll die."

Muirin's eyes flared. "You cannot stay there."

"I can," I snapped.

"You're draining your magic every second by being there," Muirin said. "That explains why you're so much weaker than before."

Ouch.

I flinched, but couldn't say anything because he wasn't wrong.

"You mean she's usually *more* powerful than this?" Conall asked.

Muirin nodded. "At least twice as much."

Four pairs of eyes glared at me.

Muirin closed his eyes, his body began to glow, the palace shook, and then everything stilled. He opened his eyes and smirked.

I wasn't sure I liked that. What had he done?

"You have a new home, here, in my waters," Muirin said.

I glared at him. "No, thank you."

"This doesn't count towards one of my debts," he said. "I'm doing this because my boys adore you, and you need a proper home."

"I—"

Muirin gave me a hard glare that had my throat dried up and a lump in the middle.

Phelan leaned over and whispered, "It's best if you just say thank you when he's like this."

He was probably right.

"Thank you," I said.

"Can we see it?" Conall asked.

Muirin stood. "Yes, let's take Uschi to her new home."

"Good job, Dad! You got her name right," Conall praised the god and patted his shoulder.

Muirin wrapped his arm around Conall's neck and put his son in a choke hold. "Impertinent, child."

CHAPTER THIRTEEN

"I can't accept this," I gasped as I stood in the center of a huge mansion beneath the sea.

He'd created it so that there was no water inside of the house. And, there were eight rooms, plus a bathroom with plumbing, and fey lanterns run off of fey magic, which would not run out for a hundred years at least.

"You can and you will accept it," Muirin said.

"It's too much. Too big. Too—" I gaped as I took in the workshop, which he'd stocked with supplies, a giant cauldron, and several newer human inventions.

"You've made her speechless," Wolfram whispered. "I didn't think that was possible."

I would have been mad, but I hadn't thought it was possible either.

"How close is this to your place?" Phelan asked.

Muirin smiled, but didn't respond.

"What's the catch?" I asked and folded my arms across my chest.

All eyes turned to Muirin.

He laughed. "There's no catch."

I arched one of my eyebrows.

Muirin snapped his fingers and the boys disappeared. "One catch."

I dropped my arms and laughed while shaking my head. "I knew it."

He stepped closer to me and whispered, "Just give my boys a chance. I've not seen them interested in a woman like this before. They care about you, all of them. They don't usually have something that unites them, but you, you have united them in ways I only dreamed of."

"I am giving them a chance. That's why I'm here on this trip with them," I said.

"You care about them, too," he said. Not a question, a statement.

I nodded.

"Is it strange that for the first time I don't have the urge to warn someone not to treat my boys badly, but want to beg you to just give them a chance? I think that means something, Uschi. You and them fit together. You all look good together," Muirin said and smiled. "If you want to bind them to you, I give my consent."

My mouth dropped. "Bind them to me? It's a bit early to discuss that."

"I know, but I wanted to tell you now anyway. I am certain the idea will come up sooner than you think," he said and winked at me.

Four large seals swam into the front entrance, eyes trying to bore holes into the god beside me.

"Ah, they've returned," Muirin said. "Shall we return to my place? You can finish your dinner and then either stay the night or set sail after."

The brothers shifted, still glaring.

"What did he talk to you about?" Wolfram asked.

"None of your business," Muirin said. He snapped his fingers again, teleporting the boys away.

I laughed. "They're going to be so mad."

He opened a portal and said, "Sometimes, a father must annoy his children. It's for their own good."

I stepped through the portal, back into Muirin's living room, and took back my spot on the fur rug, sighing as the fireplace warmed me.

Muirin sat in his chair, drinking what looked like coffee.

"Can I have hot chocolate?" I requested.

Muirin snapped his fingers and a steamy cup of hot chocolate with a big swirl of whipped cream appeared beside me.

I picked it up and squealed. "I haven't had this in a decade at least."

"Really, Dad?" Phelan demanded as the foursome marched into the room.

I grinned like a kid in a candy shop and took a tiny sip of the cocoa so I wouldn't burn my tongue or lips.

"What are you drinking?" Conall asked as he sat beside me.

"Hot chocolate," I said and scooped some of the whipped cream from the mug with my finger, and then licked it off. "So good," I moaned and closed my eyes.

"What's the plan?" Wolfram asked.

"Stay the night here, then sail out in the morning," I said. "If that works for you guys?"

They all nodded. "That's fine with us."

"That means more bagpipes in the morning for me," I said and smiled wide.

"Yay," the four guys chorused in the most sarcastic tones I had ever heard.

"Don't mind them. They're just teasing you. They all like the bagpipes a lot," Muirin said.

"A lot is an exaggeration," Phelan said. "We can stand them, but we don't like them."

"Really?" Muirin asked with an arched brow. "Care to make a wager?"

"What kind of wager?" Wolfram asked.

"If I can prove to Uschi that you love the bagpipes before you leave tomorrow, you owe me a month of being my errand boys," Muirin said.

"If we win?" Conall asked.

Muirin motioned at the guys, who followed him to the far side of the room.

I sipped on my treat while I watched them stick their heads close while Muirin told them his offering.

All of their eyes widened, they turned to look at me, and then looked back at their dad and held out their hands to shake them.

I narrowed my eyes at Muirin. What had he promised them?

The men took their seats again while I gave Muirin my best glare, still drinking my cocoa.

"So, how do you expect to win?" Marrok asked.

"A god does not reveal his tricks," Muirin said. Something popped into existence in his hand, and he held it out towards my drink.

I moved my drink back and put my hand over the top of it. "What is it?"

"Alcohol," Muirin said smirking. "Your favorite kind for cocoa."

My eyes widened and I held the mug out as far as I could. "Please."

He unscrewed the lid on the alcohol and let two tiny drops fall into my mug.

I glared at him and shook the mug.

"Do you remember the last time you drank this?" he asked with an arched brow.

I shook it again.

He sighed and put two more drops.

"Spoon?" I asked.

He handed me one and then shook the bottle at the guys. "You four interested?"

"What is it?" Wolfram asked.

"Booze," I said. "Don't be a bunch of babies. Drink."

"Did she call us babies?" Phelan asked.

"Are you challenging us to a drinking competition?" Wolfram asked.

"You would not stand a chance," Muirin said. "She'll drink you under the table."

I smiled proudly.

"Oh, no. I see what you're doing," Marrok said and stood up. "You're trying to get us drunk."

Muirin chuckled. "No, I didn't challenge you to anything. She did." He pointed at me.

"It's fine. You baby demigods can just sit there while the adults drink," I said. I clinked my mug against the bottle Muirin held. "Cheers."

Muirin saluted me and took a swig while I took a sip of my cocoa. It burned in a new way as it went down, and immediately I felt warmth building in my stomach.

"Toasty," I whispered.

Muirin and I looked at the boys with wide smiles.

"Do you guys want me to tuck you in before I continue drinking?" I asked them. "We left your baby blankets on the ship, though."

Muirin laughed so loud that the palace shuddered.

Wolfram stood, grabbed a glass from the table, and held it out towards Muirin.

The others followed suit.

"You sure about this?" Muirin asked. "This isn't like the swill you drink from the humans."

"Pour," Wolfram barked.

Muirin poured four drops into the cup. "There, now you have as much as she does."

The others followed suit.

I held up my mug. "Cheers," I said with a wicked smile.

"Don't drink it all at once," Muirin cautioned them. "Sip it like she is."

Muirin's four sons downed their cups in one drink.

Muirin's smile was so wide and warm, I felt the heat on my skin.

"Let's go somewhere fun," Muirin said. "We should take Uschi to your favorite place."

"Goldie's?" Conall asked with wide eyes.

Muirin nodded.

"Let's go!" Conall said.

I clutched my mug. "I'm not done drinking yet," I said.

"You can bring it," Muirin promised. "Goldie is a friend and won't mind you drinking it."

Muirin opened a portal and the boys leapt through.

"This was your plan all along, wasn't it?" I asked. "You were going to get them drunk to admit to liking bagpipes."

"Oh, there's so much more fun to be had, Uschi. Just wait." Muirin laughed, linked arms with me, and tugged me through the portal.

We stepped into a rowdy bar that seemed to be made even rowdier by the four men on stage, singing a Scottish drinking song. I was stunned into open-mouthed silence as I listened to them.

The four were swaying from side to side, beer in one hand

each, and huge smiles on their faces as they sang with beautiful voices.

"Why do you keep acting surprised when they do something well? They're my sons," Muirin said.

I followed him to the bar, taking sips from my mug. "I just found out today that they are yours," I said. "And not all demigods take after their godly parents."

He chuckled. "I'll not tell Poseidon you meant him."

I rolled my eyes. "He isn't the only one."

The guys started singing another song and some other drunk men joined them on stage.

I chuckled and leaned against the bar while I drank my cocoa which was cooling down. I needed to drink it faster.

"What's that you brought into my bar?" a woman with a thick brogue asked.

"She's with me, Goldie," Muirin said.

I didn't take my eyes off the guys, trusting Muirin to deal with the owner.

"Your boys prowling for women?" Goldie asked.

I tensed.

"No," Muirin said. "They've got all they want already."

A leggy redhead approached the stage, and the guys all stared.

Jealousy reared its head, but I kept my seat, sipping on my drink.

Phelan talked to the woman, a huge smile on his face, and she tossed her hair as she laughed at something he said.

The mug's handle groaned in my hold.

"Green doesn't suit you," Wolfram whispered in my ear.

I loosened my grip and took another sip before responding. "I don't know what you're talking about."

He took my mug, set it in Muirin's hand, and pulled me up. "Dance with me."

"We danced earlier," I said, pressing a hand to his chest. He was so drunk.

Bagpipes began to play from the stage. I peeked around him and my eyes widened at the redhead and two other women playing the bagpipes.

"You thought I was flirting with her, didn't you?" Phelan asked as he strutted towards me.

I scoffed and turned my head. "I don't care what you do."

He pulled me away from Wolfram and said, "Then you won't mind if I do this." He kissed me, and then spun us into a dance around the room.

People scurried out of our way, and I laughed loudly, my stomach warming and the alcohol beginning to kick in.

"I thought you hated bagpipes?" I asked.

He smiled. "You love them, though. They make you smile. And, I love seeing you smile."

Wolfram stole me from Phelan. "My turn."

I kissed his cheek as we danced, and he gave me a wide smile.

Conall snagged me next and kissed me. A drunk human fell over in our path, and Conall picked me up as he jumped over the man, doing a spin as he did, and making it look like it was part of our dance.

I expected Marrok to take me next, but Muirin stole me.

"Hey!" four male voices protested.

Muirin laughed. "I haven't had this much fun in years."

I hadn't either.

"Get them to say they love bagpipes and I'll give you anything you want."

My eyes widened. "Anything?"

Marrok tried to steal me, but Muirin spun us the opposite way, making Marrok miss and fall onto a table.

"Anything."

"What did you tell them you'd give them? I know it had to do with me."

"That's what you want for your bargain?" Muirin asked, smirking.

I growled at him. "Muirin."

"Knowledge about you that could benefit them in their pursuit of you," he said.

I arched a brow.

He laughed. "I never specified what it was."

"Anything I want?" I asked again.

He nodded.

"Deal," I said.

Muirin spun me in place, and Marrok took me from him.

"Hey," I said, smiling wide.

He smiled back. "Hi."

"So, you like this music?" I asked.

Marrok shrugged. "It's okay, but the view is phenomenal."

I laughed and shook my head. "Flirt."

He smiled. "I love your smile."

"You know bagpipes make me smile," I said.

He nodded.

"So, since you love my smile, that means you love bagpipes because they cause the smile," I said.

He frowned a moment and said, "I guess you're right. I love bagpipes."

The music stopped and Muirin yelled, "Victory!"

Marrok groaned and then glared at me. "You tricked me."

I stood on tiptoe and kissed him. "Sea witch, remember?"

The music started again, and the humans resumed dancing.

He chuckled and kissed me. "You're going to pay for that."

"Spankings?" I asked with a wink.

He groaned and pulled me tighter against his body, letting me feel just how that question affected him. "Don't tease me."

I turned and danced in front of him. "Promises, not teasing."

He watched me with lust making his eyes glow and the erection in his pants flex.

I backed away from him, swinging my hips to the music.

I ran into someone, and turned, expecting to find one of the guys, but instead found Hades, Greek God of the Underworld.

He glared down at me and before I could open my mouth, he grabbed me by the throat and tossed me through a portal.

"Uschi!" Marrok yelled, but it was too late.

CHAPTER FOURTEEN

"What do you want, Hades?" I asked, rubbing at my throat.

Moans, wails, and screams came from the other end of the cave we stood in.

We were in one of the cave entrances to the Underworld. I'd been here a few times, most of them because I brought someone back to life and that made Hades angry.

"You've disobeyed me, again," he yelled.

Cerberus stepped around the corner, his three heads growling loudly.

I stood, ignored Hades, and walked to Cerberus, crooning and calling him cute names. He stopped growling and his giant tail wagged behind him.

I scratched beneath his chins and got soaked with three giant dog tongues licking me.

Hades sighed. "Please stop doing that. He's a hellhound, not a dog."

"He's a good boy. The bestest boy. He deserves all the praise," I said in a sweet voice. "Even hellhounds need affection."

Hades sighed again and rubbed at his temples. "Look! You're in big trouble," he growled.

I hopped onto Cerberus's center head and scratched behind his ears. "Where's Persephone? Take me to her."

Cerberus took off at a trot with me holding onto his neck with my legs for balance. Hades roared behind us.

The palace came into view, and I spotted Persephone in her grove. Cerberus dropped me off at the grove and before I could say anything, Persephone hugged me.

"SuSu!" she yelled. "It's been so long. Wait. Why are you here? Did my husband snatch you again?"

Hades stepped out of the shadow to our right. "Blossom, it's not what you think."

"He stole me while I was dancing with some guys," I told Persephone with a pout.

Her mouth dropped open, and she turned to glare at the God of the Underworld. "Take her back, now!"

"After I talk to her. She's been bad," Hades said.

Persephone rolled her eyes. "She's a sea witch, so of course she has. You usually enjoy when she's bad."

"She keeps resurrecting a pirate who belongs to me," Hades snapped.

I crossed my arms over my chest. "Blackleg is *mine*."

Hades began to glow and dark tendrils spread from him. "I am the ruler of—"

Persephone poked his chest, knocking him back a step. She was barely over five feet tall, and not strong, but her husband was wrapped around her finger. "Don't you go god on her. She saved me, twice. She has helped you lots. Let her keep her friend."

"Blossom," Hades began, but she folded her arms across her chest and glared. Her glares weren't scary in the slightest. The

Goddess of Spring was the most adorable woman ever, and Hades loved her unconditionally.

The glare wasn't working, so she stuck her lip out in a pout and her plump, pink lip quivered. "She's my friend, Hades."

My jaw dropped. One, I'd never been called a friend by anyone. God or otherwise. Two, she very rarely lied, so she meant it. We had a past, but knowing she thought of me as a friend, now, still, made my eyes water.

Hades sighed and then groaned. "Fine. Fine! Keep your damn pirate. But no more."

I made an x over my heart.

Persephone hugged me and kissed my cheek. "See, he can be reasonable sometimes."

"Thank you," I whispered to her.

"Now, take her back to her date," Persephone ordered Hades. Her lips pursed and she said, "Wait, take me with you so I can see proof you released her."

Hades bristled. "You are not going to a human bar."

"Just open the portal and I'll step through," I suggested.

Persephone nodded. "What she said."

Hades glared at me but opened the portal.

I stepped through, but stepped back and waved to Persephone. "Bye, Seph."

She waved with a wide smile. "Bye, SuSu! Come see me soon."

I stepped through and found the bar completely trashed and several humans injured.

"Uschi!" Marrok yelled.

Arms wrapped around me and picked me up.

"What happened?" I asked.

"They flipped out when Hades took you," Muirin said.

I turned in Marrok's hold and found Phelan, Conall, and Wolfram knocked out at Muirin's feet.

"I was putting them to sleep to stop them," Muirin explained.

"What happened?" Marrok asked. "Did he hurt you?"

"Nothing happened. Hades was just being himself," I said.

Muirin opened a portal and tossed the unconscious guys through. Marrok followed while carrying me.

Marrok sat on the fur rug in Muirin's living room and cradled me in his lap. "I thought I was going to have to fight my way through the Underworld to get you back," Marrok whispered and kissed my cheek.

I jerked back and stared, wide eyed. "Don't you ever consider such a thing!"

He glared at me. "Why wouldn't I?"

"You wouldn't survive in the Underworld. You would die. Promise me you won't ever go to the Underworld until you're actually dead," I said.

"If he takes you—"

"Hades and I have a friendly relationship. He's mad because I keep resurrecting Blackleg," I said. "Persephone likes me and she's the reason I came back so soon. Normally, he keeps me down there a couple days to scold me, but he won't kill me."

"You can't be sure. Gods are often—"

"Gods are often what?" Muirin asked.

Marrok flinched. "Unpredictable," he said.

"Muirin, forbid him from ever going to the Underworld until he dies," I said, turning to face him.

"If I forbid him, it will make it more appealing," Muirin said.

I groaned and stood, slapping at Marrok's hands as he tried to keep me in his lap.

Conall, Wolfram, and Phelan sat up with groans.

"Uschi!" Wolfram yelled and tried to stand, but staggered. "We have to get Uschi!"

"I'm right here," I said, walking over to them.

"Uschi!" the three of them yelled.

I stopped and watched as they fumbled, crawled, and pushed each other in their attempt to get to me quickly.

Wolfram was first, and he hugged me tightly. "Are you okay? Did that bastard hurt you?"

"I'm fine, guys. You don't need to worry about Hades and I," I said and patted his back.

"I think everyone needs to get some rest," Muirin said. "I've got rooms made up for each of you."

Conall pulled me from Wolfram and kissed my cheeks. "I'm sorry we weren't close enough to grab you."

"You guys, I—"

Phelan took me next, hugging me tightly. "Do you know how far the Underworld's entrance is from here? It would have taken us months to get there."

I groaned and pushed back so I could look at all of the men in the palace at once. "You are never, ever, to come to the Underworld after me. Do you understand? If you do, and manage to rescue me or whatever, I'll stop speaking to you."

Wolfram slid his hand along my cheek and said, "As long as you were safe, it would be worth it."

I groaned, walked to the nearest wall and banged my head against it. "Stubborn. Idiotic. Men. Don't. Understand. Anything."

Marrok pulled me away from the wall. "Stop that."

Truthfully, it warmed my heart to know that they were willing to go to such lengths for me. It also terrified me.

"I'm going to bed," I said softly. "Thank you for tonight."

"Uschi," Wolfram called after me.

I didn't stop or turn around. I needed a moment. If I didn't get a moment to myself, I was going to have a breakdown in front of them.

"Leave her, she's tired. Going to the Underworld does that to a person," Muirin said.

He was covering for me, and I was thankful.

I went to the first guest room I could find, shut and locked the door behind me, and slumped down against the door.

They were going to go to the Underworld for me. They were planning to fight Hades, a god, for me.

What was wrong with them? I wasn't worth that. I wasn't worth their deaths.

I'd never had anyone care about me so much before. Not even my own parents had cared that much.

Muirin teleported into my room.

I scowled at him. "What if I was naked?"

He smiled. "Then I'd be getting a wonderful eyeful."

Laughing, I stood. "What do you want?"

"I want to tell you not to push them away. Their devotion is frightening to you, but it shouldn't be. It should be proof that they're worth it. They're worth giving a chance."

"They were going to die for me," I said. "If they'd gone to the Underworld..." I couldn't even finish that statement.

"They may not realize it yet, I know you haven't realized it yet, but you love each other. If you push them away, if you toss their love away, you're going to die alone and miserable. If you let them, if you just give them a chance to prove they can make you happy, your future is bright," Muirin said.

"Did you foresee that?" I asked.

He shook his head. "I don't need to be a god to see that. Even a human could see it. Love like this doesn't happen often."

"There are four of them," I said and scoffed.

"Yet you love them all equally."

Damn him, he was right. I wouldn't say that out loud though.

"I won't run from them," I promised.

He nodded. "Good."

"I know what I want for helping you win the bet with them," I said.

Muirin tensed and folded his arms across his chest. "Okay."

"I want something, a stone or object of some sort, that I can use to teleport them back here if we're in a dangerous situation," I said.

Muirin scowled. "They'll skin me alive if I give you something like that. If you send them here while you're in peril, they'll hate me."

"You said I could have anything," I reminded him.

He growled. "Fine."

"Make it jewelry or something I can keep on me at all times," I said.

"Promise me you'll give them a legitimate chance at becoming your husbands. Promise me that, and I'll make the item for you," Muirin said and held out his hand.

I shook it, sealing the deal. "Done."

He gripped my hand. "These are selkies, don't forget that."

I frowned. "What is that supposed to mean?"

"It means when you *seal* a deal, it has even more weight to it," he said and smirked.

I laughed and shook my head. "A pun. I didn't take you for someone who enjoyed puns."

He shrugged and released my hand. "It's not often I get to make a seal pun."

"Well, now that we've *sealed* our deal, how about you leave me so I can get some sleep. It's been a busy day," I said.

He disappeared, and I shook my head.

"Sealing the deal," I murmured then chuckled.

CHAPTER FIFTEEN

After a delicious breakfast, Muirin took us to the docks to see us off.

He'd given the guys a bunch of provisions, and they were taking them below deck for storage.

Muirin turned to me and held out a golden upper arm cuff. "This is the item you requested."

"How do I make it work?" I asked.

"You have to get one of them to hold it, or put it on one of their arms. Then you just say, 'sealed,' and it will teleport them."

I smirked. "Punny and useful. I like it."

His smile disappeared, and he scowled down at me. "Please, don't use it unless it is a last resort and it is to save my boys. I don't want them to die, but I don't want them to hate me the rest of their lives because you died either."

I slid the cuff on, and smiled at him. "I promise."

"Uschi!" Wolfram called. "Time to go."

Muirin hugged me. "Take care of my boys."

"I'll try," I said. "They're a handful though."

He laughed. "You're telling me! You should have seen what it was like raising those four."

I waved to him as I boarded the ship, this time they'd dropped a plank for me to walk up at least.

Wolfram pulled it up as soon as I was onboard, and they set sail.

"What's that?" Phelan asked, pointing at my arm cuff.

"A gift from your father. He said I deserved one for putting up with you guys," I said and smiled wide. Without waiting for the follow up questions I was certain would come, I headed to the bow of the ship, leaning my elbows on the railing as we made our way back out into the ocean.

"Don't forget to grab a coat from your quarters," Wolfram called. "We're going to be traveling through some really cold waters soon."

I climbed over the railing and sat on the forepeak. "I'll worry about that when it starts to get cold," I called back.

They called orders to each other as we sailed, and I replayed the events of the past day.

They loved me. I loved them.

I wasn't sure which was more shocking.

Okay, I was totally sure the fact that they loved me was more shocking, but still. Absorbing that information was difficult.

I hadn't been in love before. I'd thought I was in love once, but it hadn't been love. It had been infatuation.

Was that what this was, too? I'd yet to sleep with any of them, so it was a possibility.

But people didn't usually travel to the Underworld to rescue each other when it was just infatuation. That was when they would realize that they didn't actually love them.

"You're scowling rather hard," Conall said.

"Processing some information I received," I said. "It's just difficult for me to accept."

"Want to talk about it?" he asked.

Yes, but there was no way I could do that.

"Maybe another time," I said softly.

"You know, you can talk to us about whatever you want. We wish you would talk to us more," he said.

"I'm not used to having anyone to talk to," I admitted. "It's going to take some time for me to get used to having people I can share things with. I'll try though, okay?"

He smiled. "That's the best I could hope for."

"I'm sorry you lost the bet with your dad," I said.

He climbed over the railing and sat beside me. "He would have won no matter what. Dad never loses."

"He is a god," I said and laughed.

"What did you win from him for helping us?" Conall asked.

I raised my arm. "This pretty piece of jewelry."

"Really? That's all you asked for? You could have gotten something really cool or powerful from him I bet," he said.

"I just wanted this pretty arm cuff," I said and stroked it with my fingertip. I felt the magic coursing within it and smiled.

"It looks good on you," he said and smiled. "Do you like jewelry? You don't usually wear any."

"I love jewelry, but this is actually the first piece that I've been given. I have jewelry from deals I've made, but I never felt like wearing those," I said. It was weird to admit that.

"So, if I were to buy you something, you would wear it?" he asked with a smirk.

I nodded. "Yes."

He nodded back. "Noted."

We lapsed into silence, watching the waves and feeling the breeze on our faces.

As Wolfram had said, it wasn't long until it started to get cold.

I began to shiver and rubbed at my arms. "Maybe I'll get that jacket now."

Conall helped me over the railing, and I hurried to my cabin, grabbing the furry jacket Muirin had given me.

"Before you put that on," Marrok said behind me.

I turned around with the jacket in my arms.

He shut the door and locked it.

I arched a brow. "Yes?"

He stalked towards me, and I could see him being a panther instead of a seal. His eyes never left mine as he slid his hands to my waist and pulled me closer. "Uschi, I've been dying to touch you for the past week," he breathed. He kissed me and I kissed him back, letting our tongues tangle as we did.

I dropped the jacket, my hands going to his shirt and tugging on it.

He stepped back, jerked his shirt off, took my hands, and placed them on his sculpted chest. Demigods were always ripped. Marrok was no exception.

He tugged on my shirt.

"You sure about this?" I asked, swallowing and ignoring the voice in my head calling me a moron. "Your brothers might get jealous."

He pulled my shirt off over my head, and stared down at my bare chest. "I'm positive about this, and they'll be jealous, but I don't care. I want you. I wanted you when we met you, I wanted you last night in the bar, and I want you now."

The bulge in his pants was proof of that.

"I can't have children," I said softly

He frowned. "What?"

"I can't have children. I'm infertile."

He nodded. "Okay."

"That doesn't ruin this for you? That you could end up with me long term and not have children?"

He shook his head. "I've never wanted kids. None of us

have." He bent closer to me and whispered in my ear, "Plus, being with you long term is worth any price."

"Don't say that," I whispered. "Gods might hear you and—"

"Uschi," he whispered and turned my head with his finger. "Shut up and kiss me."

I did, and the feel of our naked chests together was glorious. My core clenched as he slid his hands down to grip my butt.

"If you don't want to do this, just tell me," he whispered. "I'll leave right now."

I slid my hand into his pants and gripped his erection. "I want this. I want it inside me."

He pulled my pants down, then his, and carried me to the bed. "That can be arranged."

He lay me down, spread my legs so he could fit between them, and then slid inside of me.

I moaned and arched up.

He moaned, too. "Uschi, you're so wet."

The urge to make a pun or joke about being from the sea was strong, but I held back. "I've wanted you for a long time, too," I said.

He lowered himself to his elbows and kissed me. "You're beautiful, extraordinary, and I'm going to remember this moment the rest of my life."

He pumped his hips, and I arched up again with a gasp. "No pressure," I said and chuckled, my voice breathy.

He moaned as he increased his rhythm and leaned up. His warm hands stroked my breasts and squeezed them.

"These are perfect," he said and leaned down to kiss each of my breasts. "Perfectly round. Perfectly shaped. Perfectly sized." He sucked on one nipple, making me gasp, and then sucked on the other. "I've never seen boobs so perfect."

"Says the demigod with the perfectly sculpted body," I said. "I'm sure you've seen lots of boobs."

He nodded. "I have, which is why I can say for certain that you have the perfect boobs." He squeezed them. "So soft." He growled and then pounded into me fast and hard, our skin slapping together with each stroke. "Yes. Yes," he panted.

Glorious pressure built within me and then spilled over in a tidal wave of pleasure. I screamed my orgasm, my muscles tightening around him.

He grunted and then orgasmed, too.

He lay down, half on me, and still inside me, and panted. "I did not mean to finish so soon."

I chuckled. "You were perfect."

"Uschi, I'm sorry about last night."

I pushed back his hair so I could see his face. "What are you talking about?"

"About letting Hades take you," he said.

I shook my head and kissed the tip of his nose. "You couldn't have prevented a god from taking me."

"I could have tried," he said.

I shook my head. "No, but I do appreciate that you were willing to attempt to rescue me. I've never had someone willing to rescue me before."

He stroked my cheek softly with the back of his hand. "I'd travel to the ends of the earth and back, to the Underworld, to Mount Olympus, wherever I had to go, to get you back."

My breath hitched.

"I love you, Uschi," he whispered and kissed me lightly on the lips.

"I love you, too, Marrok," I whispered.

He smiled and kissed me deeply.

Someone knocked on the door. "Get her dressed," Phelan said. "We're entering the cold zone."

Marrok stood, grabbed a towel from one of the drawers, and handed it to me.

I used it to clean myself, and then quickly got dressed and put on the jacket.

Marrok dressed as well, but didn't have a jacket.

"Aren't you going to be cold?" I asked.

He shook his head. "We like the cold."

I headed towards the door, but he grabbed me and pulled me back for another kiss.

"Say it again," he whispered.

I smiled. "I love you."

He smiled back. "I love you, too."

My heart soared, and I hugged him tightly.

He slid an arm around my shoulders and tucked me against his side. "Come on, let's go look at the pretty ice and snow."

We stepped outside, and he led me to the helm where his other brothers were.

I shivered despite having the jacket and Marrok with me. "Dang, it is cold."

Conall came on my other side and put an arm around my waist. "It's going to get colder still," he said.

"You slept with her," Conall shouted.

I cringed.

Marrok smiled proudly, keeping his arm around me. "Yep."

"Cheater," Conall grumbled. "I thought we were going to wait."

"Wait until what?" I asked.

Conall froze and looked down at me, apparently just remembering I was still there. "Um, until we'd gotten to the Pacific."

I arched a brow. "Has anyone ever told you that you're a terrible liar?"

"All the time," all of his brothers said simultaneously.

I laughed and tugged Conall closer to me. "Come keep me warm. You can keep your plans about seducing me secret still."

CHAPTER SIXTEEN

I'd never been to oceans with ice before. I marked it on my lists of things never to do again.

I was infinitely grateful for the guys' choice to sail on a ship instead of swimming now. Had I been subjected to swimming in the water, I doubted I would have survived long.

My breath formed clouds in front of me every time I breathed. "So cold," I objected and shivered.

Conall, Marrok, and Phelan were crowded around me, their hands rubbing up and down me to try to warm me up.

"How long will I be subjected to this?" I asked.

"At least two days," Wolfram said.

"Screw that!" I snapped and pushed away from the guys. I marched to the stern of the ship and gathered my magic. I was not going to sail slowly through this crap. I leaned through the railing and slapped my hand on the wood just above the captain's cabin's windows.

The ship groaned, the water below it glowed, and then it surged forward.

My shoulder got twisted and I was glad I hadn't leaned over

the railing to do it, because I likely would have fallen into the icy water.

I stood, rubbing my sore shoulder, and smiled. "That should help."

Marrok, Conall, and Phelan stood just a foot away from me, scowling.

"What?" I asked.

"They were worried you were going to fall in," Wolfram called from the helm. "They were arguing about who got to shift and save you."

"Where do you keep your pelts?" I asked. It was something I had been curious about for a while. Unlike other shifters, they used their seal pelts to shift. If they didn't have them, they couldn't turn into seals.

Their eyes widened, and I saw fear there.

I waved my hand and walked by them. "Never mind. Forget I asked. I don't want to know."

Truthfully, their fear hurt me. At this stage, they still thought I might use the information against them.

I sat on the railing in front of the wheel and curled my legs up so I could wrap the jacket around them. I blew out white air and used my magic to shape it into two men fighting.

The guys sat on the railing around me, watching the wispy men battle each other.

Phelan reached out and swiped away one of the men's legs and my conjured creation stumbled, using his sword to keep him upright. It turned and had I given it eyes, it would have glared at Phelan.

"That is creepy," Conall whispered.

I blew out a long breath and turned it into dog-like monsters who joined the battle. The one-legged man killed one of the dogs and then swiped the cloudy creature so he could create a leg for himself.

"Whoa," Marrok whispered, his eyes wide.

"Could you create something like that with a physical form?" Wolfram asked behind me from his spot at the wheel.

"Without having a dead body to reanimate?" I asked.

"Yes," he answered.

"Maybe. I've never tried before," I said. "Hades hates it when I steal souls from him."

"Is that why he stole you the other night? Because of Black-leg?" Wolfram asked.

I nodded. I added more creatures to the fray and more men and pushed them back so the fighting would be easier to watch.

Something slammed into the side of the boat, knocking me off balance. I started to fall, but Marrok and Phelan grabbed each of my arms and kept me on the railing.

"What was that?" I asked. Hopping down once the guys freed my arms, I marched towards the side of the boat, but stayed far enough back that if we got rammed again, I wouldn't fall in.

I watched as a large black and white whale sped towards us and rammed the boat again.

"Our enemy," Phelan spat. "Killer whales."

"Your enemy?" I asked with an arched brow. "It's a whale."

"Their favorite meal is seal," Conall said. "He probably smells us on the ship."

Ah. That explained it.

I pushed the sleeves of my jacket up and raised my hands in the air. The cold air swirled above my hands and solidified into a spear of ice. I handed the spear to Phelan.

I gave him a wide smile. "Happy hunting."

Phelan gave me a predatory smile, kissed my cheek, and then hopped up on the railing. The whale sped towards the side of the ship again and Phelan launched the spear.

It hit true, and the whale made a high-pitched noise that

hurt my ears, red flooded the waters, and it disappeared from sight.

"There's never just one," Conall said.

I created ten more spears and the guys grabbed them out of the air.

Wolfram yelled, "Uschi, come steer so I can hunt, too."

I skipped up the steps and took the wheel.

Marrok tossed Wolfram a spear and I watched as my handsome selkie demigods took their rage out on whales attempting to sink us to eat them. I'd never thought of seals as true predators before since they usually just ate fish and penguins, but watching them changed my opinion.

"Panthers," I said loud enough for them to hear.

"What?" they asked in unison, watching the dead whales floating behind us.

If there were sharks in these cold waters, they would surely consume them soon enough.

"Had you been born shifters of any other species, you four would have been panthers," I said.

Something shimmered ahead of us and I squinted as I tried to make out what it was.

"There's something in the water," I called.

"Probably ice," Wolfram said.

"It's shiny," I called back.

They jogged up to me and Marrok ran past me to look over the figurehead.

"Iceberg!" Marrok yelled.

Too late. It was too late.

Wolfram tried to steer the ship around it, but the iceberg was much larger below the surface than it looked and our ship crashed into it. The impact sent everyone flying but luckily, we all stayed on the ship, even Marrok.

"We're sinking!" Marrok yelled.

"No, we're not!" I snapped and ran below deck. It didn't take me long to find the giant hole and water was quickly filling the ship.

I groaned but dove into the icy water, instantly hating it and shivering. I used my magic to push us away from the iceberg and used the water to create an ice wall patch.

My eyelids grew heavy and I was shaking so badly that I couldn't see straight.

A seal swam in front of me and snapped its teeth.

I tried to glare at it, but moving anything was becoming impossible. I'd transformed at some point and tried to use my tentacles to swim, but they were covering in ice.

Something was wrong. The water shouldn't have been that cold. I should have been able to withstand it longer. Octopi could live in freezing cold water for a time.

This was magical.

The seal pushed me with his head, moving me back towards the stairs.

The water. I had to do something with the water before I passed out.

With the little strength I had left, I focused on the water and sent it up in a huge water spout out of the stairwell.

Then, the world went dark.

"Wake up, dammit. Wake up, Uschi," Wolfram growled at me. "We need you. Wake up! You damn, stubborn, opinionated, sea witch!"

Someone was pushing on my chest and it hurt.

I sat up, gasped and then immediately puked water.

I was on the deck of the ship with the guys standing around me and Wolfram squatted next to me.

"I never thought I'd be able to drown before," I said. "I can breathe underwater."

"Not when a spell freezes your gills shut," Wolfram whispered.

Spell?

I leapt to my feet, staggered, and put my hand on Marrok's shoulder. He and the other three faced away from me. "What's going on?"

"You've invaded our waters, sea witch," a voice I'd always hated due to the high-pitched whine, said.

I groaned and pushed around Marrok. "You little bitch. Get the fuck off my ship," I snarled.

Before me stood ten hippocampi and one angry Ceto. She and I had a long history of hatred. As the goddess of the dangers of the ocean and sea monsters, she hated when I killed her precious creatures. If her stupid creatures had stopped invading my territory, I wouldn't have had to keep killing them.

"You killed ten whales," she snapped. "Ten!"

Now was not the time to point out the guys had done the killing. "They were trying to sink my ship," I said.

"You owe me retribution," she said and folded her arms across her chest.

"You can kiss my a—"

Wolfram slapped a hand over my mouth. "They were going to sink us. We only protected the ship," he said.

She gave him a good, long look.

I tried to break free of Wolfram's hold so I could gouge out her eyes.

"One night with you would be retribution enough for my lost whales," she said and licked her lips.

I flicked my hand, causing the board beneath her foot to snap, bend upward, and smack her in the face.

She howled and the hippocampi snapped their teeth.

I bit Wolfram's hand, and he pulled it back with a yelp. Free, I pushed past him and squared off with the angry goddess.

"Get off my ship," I ordered her. "Or I'll be eating barbecued hippocampus and dancing on your corpse."

The hippocampi made a noise between a neigh and a growl.

I shifted into my larger form which had tentacles and serrated teeth. "Try me."

She scowled. "You're not usually so aggressive. This is no fun. Why are you so aggressive today?"

"She's had a rough week," Conall said. "She was kidnapped by Hades yesterday and fought two kings after being tortured by one. She needs a vacation. That's where we're taking her."

Ceto looked up until she met my eyes. "Transform. I want to talk."

"Swear on the sea you won't harm them or the ship," I said.

"I swear," she said with a nod.

I let myself shrink, but kept my serrated teeth. "What do you want to talk about?" I asked, hesitantly. Immortals were always tricky and she, no doubt, had tricks up her sleeve. But as long as she didn't hurt the guys, or try to screw them, I was fine.

"Someplace private?" she asked.

"Boys, play nice with the hippocampi," I said and led Ceto to the captain's cabin.

She shut the door behind her and asked, "Are you aware those are demigod selkies?"

I chuckled. "Very aware."

"Since when did you start dating again?"

I glared at her. "What do you really want to know?"

"I want to warn you. The seas are unbalanced. Poseidon is

off his rocker and Amphitrite can't control him. Zeus is considering intervening."

I stared at her. "Are you blaming me?"

She smiled. "You are partially to blame, but no. He's been falling into madness faster than his brothers. Being immortal has its downsides. Insanity seems to be one of them."

"Please tell me Zeus isn't considering opening the pit to put him in? He'll unleash some of the Titans if he opens it."

"I can't say more aside from commenting on how very intuitive and smart you are."

The Underworld had to have frozen over. Ceto had just complimented me.

She laughed. "The look of shocked disgust on your face is priceless. I'm capable of being objective from time to time."

"I preferred it when we fought. I knew where I stood with the angry bitch Ceto. This nice one confuses me."

She shook her head. "Keep a hold on those boys. There are a few who would love to get their hands on them."

"I'll cut their hands off," I snapped before I could stop myself.

She smiled. "What sea are you staying in now?"

"I haven't chosen yet, but Muirin made me a home in his waters. I am considering staying there," I said.

She nodded. "I'd rather you stayed out of my waters, so I'm fine with that. Consider me keeping your love for those selkies a secret as payment for you leaving my waters."

"Can you fix the hull of the ship? We hit an iceberg after battling with your damned killer whales."

She scowled. "You're pushing your luck, Urs—"

"Uschi," I said. "I go by Uschi now. And, please? I don't want us to sink when we finally hit warmer waters."

"Where are you headed?"

"Pacific," I said.

She closed her eyes, her body glowed, and I felt the ship rebalance. Then the air became hard to breathe, and I felt incredibly dizzy.

"What are you—"

Before I could finish my question, I fainted.

BODY LANGUAGE

CHAPTER SEVENTEEN

I woke with a gasp, bolting upright from where I'd been lying on the floor of the captain's cabin.

What had happened?

Ceto!

The guys!

I burst out of the door, slamming my shoulder into the frame as I ran out of the cabin. I inhaled, ready to scream for the guys, but let out the breath when I found the four of them lying on the deck.

The sun blasted me with heat, making me sweat instantly. Why was it always so hot above sea level in these places?

I ran to the closest of my guys, Conall, and checked his pulse and breathing. Both good. "Conall," I said.

Nothing.

"Conall!" I yelled.

His eyes opened and he sat up with a gasp. The others did as well.

"What happened?" Conall asked.

I looked around and realized we were no longer in freezing water. "She teleported us somewhere," I said.

"What?" Wolfram asked.

I kissed Conall quickly on the lips before darting to the railing. "I don't recognize this water." There were no land masses near us either.

"Why would she teleport us?" Phelan asked. "You guys hate each other."

"She was actually being nice," I grumbled. "People keep being nice to me. I don't like it."

"What did you say to her before she teleported us?" Wolfram asked.

"I told her we were going to the Pacific. Maybe she teleported us so we wouldn't be in her waters any longer than we already had," I said. All things considered, it was a nice gesture.

"What did she want to talk to you about?" Wolfram asked.

"She warned me that Poseidon has gone off the deep end. If Zeus steps in, he'll try to put Poseidon in the pit, which will allow the others to escape. It's a bad situation all around," I said.

"You two were ready to kill each other and now suddenly, you are friends?" Phelan asked.

I scowled at him. "I don't like it either! I don't understand why people aren't viewing me as evil anymore, but they aren't. I blame you guys."

"Us?" Phelan asked, eyes wide.

"Yes, you. Before you guys showed up in my life, I was just the evil sea witch everyone had to tolerate because I could obliterate them. Now, they're treating me like a regular person. I don't like it. I don't understand it. The harpies don't even hiss at me anymore!"

"Let me see if I understand this correctly," Marrok said. "You're upset because since meeting us, people no longer view you as the cold, evil bitch sea witch and now treat you nicely?"

"Yes," I said. Though, the way he said it made it seem like I was being a tad ridiculous.

"Why is that a bad thing?" Marrok asked. "They're finally seeing you for who you really are."

"I'm not a nice and caring being," I said.

Wolfram stalked over to me, squatted down so he could look me in the eye, and said, "You are a nice and caring being. We wouldn't be with you otherwise. You accepted that people thought you were evil and ran with it. You've done some bad shit. So, have we. You knew people weren't going to accept you as nice when you practice witchcraft. So, you took on that role and filled it extremely well. Now that people are seeing that Triton is a piece of snail sludge, and you can do good things, you're having an identity crisis. I get it. I understand and empathize. You're going to have to accept that you're not the evil sea witch anymore. You're not the evil sea witch. You're Uschi, and as long as we're with you, we'll remind you every chance we get that you don't ever have to be that cold, lonely sea witch ever again."

Tears threatened to fall and my chest felt tight with unleashed emotions. What had I done to deserve them? Why were they even here with me now?

"You deserve happiness. Everyone does," Wolfram whispered and wiped my eyes. He kissed me and whispered in my ear, "I love you, Uschi, and I'm going to try to make the rest of your life as amazing as possible to make up for the last thirty years."

I chuckled and threw my arms around his neck. "What happened to the asshole Wolfram I met?"

"He died when the sea witch died," he whispered.

"Alright, we think we're in the Pacific, but where in the Pacific?" Phelan asked.

Marrok climbed up to the nest, shielded his eyes from the sun, and looked in all directions. "I don't see any land."

"Wonderful," I muttered. I shifted my legs to my tentacles

and prepared to hop over the railing, but Wolfram snagged my arm, stopping me.

"Where are you going?" he asked.

"To see if there are any sentient beings below who can tell us where we are," I said.

"I'll go with you," he said.

I shook my head. "There are creatures here that would love to have you for a snack. No, you guys stay on the boat."

"If they can eat us, they can eat you, too," Conall said and folded his arms across his chest.

I arched a brow. "Me? You think something would be stupid enough to try to eat me, unprovoked?"

Conall's arms dropped to his side. "Good point. Proceed."

Wolfram grumbled something beneath his breath, but released me. "If you aren't back in an hour, we're going to come after you."

I kissed his cheek and then leapt over the railing and into the sea. The glorious coolness had a gasp of pleasure slipping from my throat as I plunged into the darkness. This sea was dirtier than ours and much harder to see far in.

I continued my descent, headed for the ocean floor. If there were any sentients, they'd likely be near the floor to avoid human detection.

Fish darted away, large sharks diverted their paths, and I smiled as my dark aura spread around me. The guys and others may not view me as evil, but my darkness was still there, and I prayed it would never disappear.

My tentacles touched the ocean floor and yet there was still no sign of sentient life.

"Hello," I called. "Anyone who can talk out here?"

A whale answered my call.

"Not you, you mammoth fool," I grumbled.

Pushing off from the sandy floor, I trudged along looking for signs of life. Aside from a few shipwrecks and random human trash, I found none.

Strange and slightly unnerving.

I felt like I was being watched and yet I could sense nothing aside from normal sea life.

The longer I stayed underwater, the uneasiness at being separated from the guys grew. With a big push, I propelled myself up and towards the surface.

As I approached the surface, I saw red and orange flickering overhead. We'd arrived with the sun at zenith, about noon, so it shouldn't have been sunset yet.

Which meant one thing...fire.

Using my tentacles in two bundles, I swam as fast as I could, breaking the surface and flying up out of the water several feet.

The ship was on fire, the guys were fighting several familiar faces, and if things weren't handled, the ship would sink.

I landed back in the water, created a wave larger than the ship, and caused it to break over it. The fire sizzled out, the guys all fell to the deck, and I took the opportunity to leap up onto the ship, changing my tentacles to legs so I could land on feet.

"What is going on?" I asked, standing with hands on my hips between my guys and the attackers.

The brothers got to their feet behind me, fists clenched.

The attackers stood and glared at me.

"This doesn't concern you," Hercules said.

I arched a brow. "You better simmer down that attitude, boy, or I'll have to remind you who actually defeated that hydra."

He cringed and his shoulders drooped slightly.

Hercules, Achilles, and Orion stood side by side, glaring at the brothers behind me.

It was common for demigods to fight, but usually because one of them talked poorly about the other's father. It was more common for demigods to join forces to try to defeat their crappy parents.

"Who sent you?" I asked. "Why are you here?"

"Dad sent us," Orion said.

Dad, otherwise known as Poseidon.

"Figures," I said and scoffed. "What's your goal?"

"Kill them," Hercules said and pointed behind me.

"Not going to happen," I said, bristling.

Orion scowled. "What? You're protecting them?"

I examined my fingernails and as nonchalantly as possible said, "They're mine. You try to hurt them, and I'll tear your arms off."

The three demigods looked at each other, mouths slightly agape, and then back at me.

"You actually have feelings then?" Orion asked.

I sighed and dropped my hands to look at them. "Just because your dad is an insufferable idiot and I left him doesn't mean I don't have feelings. Quite the opposite, I have a brain that functions and realizes that the gods are just powerful pieces of—"

"Pieces of what?" a deep male voice with a thick accent asked behind me as the skies filled with dark, broiling clouds and rain fell.

Uh oh.

I swallowed, turned and bowed. "Perfection," I finished with my head lowered.

Tlaloc, Aztec god of rain, thunder, and lightning, stood at the helm of the ship, a cape billowing out behind him while his upper body remained bare, showing off his tattoos.

"Who is that?" Hercules asked in a whisper out of the side of his mouth.

"No idea," Conall answered.

Tlaloc walked down the stairs towards me, and I fought the

warmth that grew between my legs. He was a fertility god, and amazing in bed. It had been at least ten years since I'd last seen him.

He stopped before me, his tan boots the only thing I could see. "Lift your head," he said.

I straightened and smiled at him. "Hi."

He arched a dark brow. "Hi? You abandon me ten years ago, enter my territory without permission, insult gods, and then the first thing you say is 'hi'?"

"Nice to see you," I added.

He looked at the demigods around me. "Demigods? Why are there demigods of two different pantheons here?"

"These ones are with me," I said and pointed to my left. "These ones were sent by my ex-boyfriend to kill the demigods with me," I said and pointed to my right.

"Which ex-boyfriend?" Tlaloc asked, glaring at the Greek demigods.

"Poseidon," I said.

Tlaloc's head whipped back to me. "Poseidon? You slept with Poseidon? Even after I warned you that he was—"

"I know. I'm sorry. You were right. I'm an idiot," I said and cringed. "I left him, though."

He exhaled loudly, his nostrils flaring wide as he did so. "That is something at least. And, you have not borne a child, which pleases and upsets me at the same time."

As a fertility god, that made sense.

"I'm sorry, but who are you?" Wolfram asked.

"I'm Tlaloc, God of Rain and Thunder, Fertility, and other things," Tlaloc said. "She and I were together until she abandoned me after a miscommunication."

My fists clenched at my sides. "Your followers were going to sacrifice me to you to ensure the rains continued for their crops to grow."

Tlaloc shrugged. "I would have brought you back to life, my dark princess. The pain would have only lasted a few minutes."

"The pain of being disemboweled, yes. I'll pass on that experience, thank you," I said and folded my arms across my chest.

"Why are you here, my dark beauty? If not to be reunited with me?" Tlaloc asked.

"Definitely not to be reunited with you," Wolfram growled.

Tlaloc turned his glare on Wolfram.

"We came on a vacation," I said. "Triton caused people to believe I was evil...eviler than I am. I finally cleared my name, but almost died a few times in the process."

Tlaloc's eyes filled with fire and lighting, his body straightened, and the skies exploded with thunder. "He dared to harm you?" he asked, his voice like thunder itself.

"Yes, but—"

"Where is he? I shall take him to Mictlantecuhtli to dismember again and again in the Underworld," Tlaloc said. The winds picked up and the boat began to sway dangerously.

"We killed him," Phelan said loud enough for Tlaloc to hear.

The ship settled, the winds died, and the sky stopped thundering, though it remained cloudy and raining.

"Good," Tlaloc said. "I may give you passage for protecting my dark princess."

"I'm not yours," I mumbled.

"And whose are you?" Tlaloc asked, folding his arms across his chest.

He'd always had impressive biceps and I found myself lost in their bulging beauty for a moment.

"She's ours," Wolfram said.

Tlaloc swiveled to look at the brothers. "You four?" he asked.

They nodded.

"You think the four of you are worthy of her? Of her dark beauty? Of her dark magic?"

"No, but we love her and she loves us," Conall said. "That's all that matters."

"Love?" Tlaloc asked, his eyes wide. He turned and looked at me. "My dark princess, tell me it isn't so. Tell me your heart has not closed itself to me."

"Damn, she gets around," Achilles said.

Tlaloc flung his hand out towards Achilles.

One moment Achilles was there, the next he was floating in the sky, skewered by several lightning bolts. One of which went through his heel.

Well, that looked painful.

Orion and Hercules took a step back, eyes wide with fear.

"Do not insult my dark princess," Tlaloc said and turned back to the brothers. "I do not find you worthy of her."

"It's not up to you," I said quickly.

"I will not allow it. They must pass my tests to be with you," he said.

I straightened, let my darkness seep out, fill my eyes, and swirl around me like a dark cyclone. "You have no say in my life. You do not get to decide. You do not have the right to allow or not allow anything."

Tlaloc dropped Achilles onto the ship and the demigod bounced off the wood then lay still. Most likely dead.

Tlaloc faced me, his power growing as he approached. "You would fight me, dark one?"

"I belong to no one," I hissed, my legs transforming to tentacles and pushing me upwards so I could meet his eyes. "I am my own woman. I make my own choices. I date, fuck, and kill whoever I want. You and every other god in this universe do not get a say in that. If I want to marry these four, then you cannot stop me. If you try...if you try to make them pass some stupid test because you think you have some right to me or my life, I will fight you. I will fight you and win, or die trying."

"You make bad decisions, my dark princess. You need to see these are not the right men for you," Tlaloc said. "They are weak and pathetic and—"

"I make my own decisions. Bad or not. You cannot and will not stop me," I said.

I took a step closer to him, but Wolfram stepped between us. "We are not good enough for her. We know this. We love her and we will do everything we can to protect her, though. You're just going to upset her and cause her to fight with you, which could lead to you hurting her. That's not something any of us wants."

Tlaloc looked long and hard at Wolfram. Then he smiled and the skies cleared. "I like you, seal boy."

I let my powers recede and sighed. Gods were such fickle creatures.

"If you're done, we have unfinished business," Hercules said.

I took a step back, grabbed Wolfram and pulled him back with me as well.

Tlaloc slowly turned to face Hercules and Orion. "You wish to join your brother?" he asked and glanced down at Achilles, whom I was certain was dead.

"We, uh—" Hercules looked at Orion and then at Achilles.

"You trespassed on my land, threatened my dark princess, and now presume to rush me so you can attack the ones she has given her heart to?" Tlaloc asked.

Lightning flashed, and then a second Aztec god appeared beside Tlaloc.

"What is going on, Tlaloc?" Mictlantecuhtli asked. Mictlantecuhtli, God of the Underworld.

Was he here because he'd heard Tlaloc say his name?

"These demigods are trespassing," Tlaloc said.

"No. No, we were just leaving," Hercules said and held up his hands.

"Take that one with you," Tlaloc said.

Hercules picked up Achilles and hopped off the ship and into the ocean.

Mictlantecuhtli turned towards me. "Tzitzimitl, what are you doing here?"

Tzitzimitl was the term for an Aztec star deity. They had painted me to look like a skeleton and used me to frighten their people at night, turning me into a demon amongst their people. It was Mictlantecuhtli's pet name for me, too.

"I'm visiting this ocean. Tlaloc interrupted me and—"

"You must come," Mictlantecuhtli said with wide eyes. "Itzpapalotl will want to see you."

Itzpapalotl was a goddess, queen of the Tzitzimitl.

"I can't. I'm—"

Mictlantecuhtli narrowed his eyes at me. "You will come."

"Can I bring them?" I asked and pointed at the guys.

"Who are they?" Mictlantecuhtli asked.

Tlaloc said, "Her consorts."

Mictlantecuhtli's eyes widened. "You took consorts? Four of them? I supposed you never were happy with just one man. Is four enough to satisfy you? I am certain there are others who would gladly join your harem."

I felt Wolfram tense next to me and smirked.

"I may take applications, but currently I am full," I said. "If you want me to come with you, I must bring them with me. And this ship, since it is my transportation."

Tlaloc scowled. "Why are you sailing? You swim faster than a ship."

"We traveled through frozen waters. I would have died if I had swum," I said.

"Frozen waters? How far have you traveled, Tzitzimitl?" Mictlantecuhtli asked with wide eyes.

"Let us take them and then they can tell us of their journeys," Tlaloc said.

CHAPTER EIGHTEEN

Tlaloc guided us to a port bustling with activity. He spoke to some of the men who tied our ship and promised to watch it.

Once our ship was safe, Tlaloc teleported our fivesome to the land of the gods, a jungle paradise.

Tlaloc's palace was opened to the jungle's animals, and next to his throne lay his favorite panther.

"Fifi," I yelled and rushed towards the panther.

She stood and tilted her head to the side as I ran at her. Her ears flattened, and she hissed, but I ignored her, threw my arms around her and rubbed my face against her face. She sniffed my hair and then purred and licked my cheek and forehead.

"Why am I not surprised to watch her run straight at a deadly creature?" Phelan asked.

I turned and sat in front of Fifi who continued to groom me. "Because you know that dark things like me."

"Are you insinuating that we're dark?" Conall asked.

I smirked and shrugged.

"The others will be here soon, so you only have a short time to explain to your consorts how to act," Tlaloc said to me.

"Right," I said and stood. "Treat them like Zeus, but without thinking they're insufferable jerks who stick their dicks in—"

"We get it," Phelan said. "You really should stop insulting the gods so much."

I smiled. "The Greeks know better than to trespass on the Aztec's territory."

"They do?" Marrok asked.

I nodded. "They tried once. They all nearly died, but Itzpapalotl—"

"Itzpapalotl decided to show the sniveling, pathetic creatures pretending to be gods, mercy," Itzpapalotl said as she entered.

I stood, rushed to stand before her, and then dropped to my knees and bowed. "Itzpapalotl."

She patted my head. "Tzitzimitl, you've been gone far too long. You promised to visit."

"I'm here now," I said and tilted my head back to look up at her.

She was the definition of exotic beauty. Raven black hair, caramel colored eyes, and skeletal bones painted on her face and arms made her into the fiercest yet most enchanting goddess I had ever seen.

She smiled at me. "I have missed you, my friend." She opened her arms and I stood into them, embracing her.

She pet my hair and whispered, "You have suffered many painful things recently. Some due to these men you have brought with you. Yet, you keep them as consorts?"

"What?" Tlaloc asked, standing from his throne and picking up the spear he kept nearby.

"They have been forgiven," I said quickly. I looked into Itzpapalotl's eyes. "Yes, I have suffered, but there is also happiness and joy that I have not felt in a very long time."

She looked over my head at the men. "Approach, consorts of Tzitzimitl."

The guys came to stand just behind me without hesitation.

Itzpapalotl pushed me to the side and went to Marrok, who stood on the end. She stared into his eyes for several moments and then nodded. "Strong and silent type. I like you. You pass."

Conall fidgeted as she came to him, but stilled when she looked into his eyes.

"The sweet one. Yes, I like you, too. You pass," Itzpapalotl said.

"Why do you gods keep thinking that you can decide anything on my behalf?" I grumbled.

She flicked her hand, and my lips sealed closed.

I struggled against the spell, but I couldn't open my mouth. Had it been anyone else, I would have attacked them for doing such a thing. Itzpapalotl was special, though, and I folded my arms across my chest and gave her my best glare.

She went to Wolfram next and only looked at him a moment before nodding. "You've learned that for the right woman, a man will become better and changes in order to become the best man he can be for the woman he loves. You pass."

She moved over to Phelan and narrowed her eyes.

Phelan shifted his weight on his feet and held her gaze, though I could see his pulse in his throat quickening.

She took a step closer to him and I tensed, prepared to attempt to defend him, but she rested her hand on his shoulder and said, "You have made mistakes, but you have learned from them and that is what is important. You pass."

"You are sure?" Tlaloc asked. "I don't think they are worthy."

Itzpapalotl turned her head and gave him a look that would have made most men wet their pants.

"Did I stutter, Tlaloc?" Itzpapalotl asked.

He sat down silently, still holding his spear, but now pouting since he couldn't use it.

Smart man.

"You pass and look hungry. So, please eat," she said and waved at a bounty of food I hadn't seen appear.

The guys walked towards the table with Itzpapalotl.

I waved my arms and tried to yell, only managing a loud mumble.

Everyone turned towards me.

I pointed at my mouth and widened my eyes.

"Could you leave her like that for a little bit longer?" Wolfram asked with a smirk. "I don't know when we'll have the chance for such silence again."

I gave him a glare and then snapped my fingers.

Dark tendrils slid up his legs like snakes and tied his legs together, making him fall over.

Itzpapalotl released the spell, allowing me to speak.

"Try to walk now, jerkfram," I said and strutted by him.

He grabbed my ankle, making me yelp and fall onto my stomach. I threw my arms out to keep my face from hitting the ground.

Tlaloc exploded with laughter and thunder boomed outside so loudly that it shook the palace.

"Stupid men," I grumbled and stood.

Wolfram stood as well and gave me a peck on the cheek before darting to the opposite side of the table to join his brothers to eat.

"They love you, dark one. Do not give that up easily. I sense hesitation in you, but this is the real thing," Itzpapalotl whispered.

"It's terrifying," I whispered.

She chuckled. "Face off against demons and ghouls and you

don't bat an eye. Have men tell you they love you and suddenly you're afraid? You have your fears mixed up."

I smiled and said, "That's what makes me interesting."

Tlaloc draped an arm around my shoulders and said, "That it does."

My consorts hyper focused on his arm, lips twitching in a snarl.

Several more gods from the Aztec pantheon joined us. I bowed to them all and exchanged pleasantries. The guys did well and when the sun began to rise, Tlaloc led us to a room where we could sleep.

The guys walked in first, and Tlaloc set a hand on my arm, holding me back a moment.

I looked up at him. "Yes?"

"The waters near the Greeks churns. It won't be long before that chaos reaches our waters. Tomorrow, when you set sail, be wary. I don't know what they are up to, but it is not good."

"You remember the prison they created?" I asked.

He scowled. "Yes."

"There is a rumor that they may attempt to seal another god in it. To do so, that requires opening it first," I said and raised my eyebrows, knowing I didn't need to finish the explanation for him to understand.

He sighed, dropped his head, and shook it. "They are such troublesome children. I shall advise the others so they are prepared."

"Thank you for your hospitality," I said and bowed.

He kissed my cheek. "You can still become my queen," he whispered. "It isn't too late, my dark princess."

I smiled and gave him a peck on the cheek. "I appreciate the offer, but we both know that we would butt heads way too much and would end up trying to kill one another."

He laughed and nodded. "You are right. Go to your

consorts, they're growing more and more jealous the longer I stand this close to you.

I turned and found the brothers standing with fierce glares aimed at us.

"Good night, demigods. Keep her safe," Tlaloc said, waved, and walked away.

I walked into the room, wishing the Aztecs had doors, and smirked nervously. "Hey."

They folded their arms across their chests.

"Well, I don't know about you guys, but I'm exhausted," I said, kicked off my shoes, and jumped onto the bed. The mattress was as soft as clouds and the blankets were super warm.

Phelan grabbed my legs and jerked me towards the end of the bed. He pulled my pants off in one move.

I sat up, eyes wide.

All four brothers stood at the end of the bed, shirtless.

My eyes widened.

"We have something to take care of first," Phelan said. "Apparently, you need to be reminded of the pleasures a demigod is capable of bestowing on you."

I licked my lips. "All four of you?"

They smiled, the same exact smile that left zero doubt they were brothers.

"Don't worry, we'll take turns to spread out your pleasure over the next several hours," Wolfram said.

"And then, you'll understand why four demigods is better than one god," Phelan said.

CHAPTER NINETEEN

AFTER SAYING OUR GOODBYES TO THE AZTECS, WE WENT TO our ship and set sail.

I lay on the deck, my body sore from our escapades that lasted five hours, well into the morning.

I fell asleep a few times, waking up to the sun spearing my eyelids.

"You look a little worn out," Conall said as he sat beside me.

"I can say that I am definitely not disappointed with my choice of four demigods instead of one god," I said with a smile. I held out my hand and Conall took it, linking our fingers together and setting my arm across his lap.

"I'm glad," Conall said, but the tone in which he said it made it sound like he was anything, but glad.

I sat up and looked at his troubled face. "What's wrong?" I asked. I pushed his hair back to see his full face.

"How many gods have you been with?" he asked.

I tensed. "What?"

"It seems like whenever we run into a group of gods, you have a history with them," he said.

Wolfram walked up behind Conall and slapped the back of his head.

"Ouch," Conall said and rubbed the spot.

"It doesn't matter who she was with before," Wolfram said.

"My past is a bit...unconventional," I said softly. "Due to my powers, gods took notice of me. Some for their own gain, some to try to kill me, and some out of curiosity."

Wolfram scowled. "Uschi, you don't—"

I held up my hand. "You need to know about me, if we're going to continue with this relationship."

"We aren't virgins either," Phelan said. "You don't have to discuss this."

"I've been with gods, goddesses, demigods, and humans," I said. "I was abandoned as a child. I sought love and attention from anywhere that I could. It wasn't until I got older that I realized most of them never even cared for me. After Poseidon, I shut down and put walls up around my heart. I didn't want to risk it...to risk the pain. Then I saw you four at that bar. And you morons tried to follow me in the Dead Sea, almost dying. I haven't been able to get you out of my mind since that night. I have enemies, ones who would love nothing more than to tear you apart right in front of my eyes to hurt me. They wouldn't care one second about you or your pain. All they want is me to suffer, to die. That was one of the reasons I was hesitant to date you. If they hurt you, or kill you, I'm not sure I'll survive that. I'll be a shell of myself and fairly certain I'll end up causing such massive destruction that the gods will be forced to intervene and kill me."

"We won't let anything happen to you, or each other," Wolfram said, dropped down to his knees, and gripped the back of my neck. "Together, we will be the strongest team in the universe."

I leaned forward and kissed him lightly on the lips.

"Poseidon is going to come for me. He wants to kill me. By being with me, you are all in danger."

"We are demigods, which means we are always in danger. Gods hate us and humans want to be us. Danger excites us," Phelan said.

I smirked up at him. "So, you're as insane as me, is what you're saying?"

He smiled. "Not *as* insane as you, but close enough."

I laughed and stood to hug Phelan. "Close enough."

Marrok yelled, "I think we are here."

"Here? Where is here? What are we doing?" I asked, trying to pull away from Phelan.

He kept an arm around my waist and squeezed. "To the treasure we're seeking," Phelan said.

"You boys just love being cryptic, don't you? I blame your father. Gods are always cryptic as shit," I said.

All four laughed and headed to the edge of the ship.

I watched with wide eyes as they pulled their seal pelts from their hips, out of an invisible bag. So, that was where the kept them? Their dad must have made the bags for them.

"Come on," Wolfram called. He put on his pelt, shifting into his seal form instantly, and leapt off the ship and into the water.

I leapt next, shifted my legs into my tentacles in midair, and sighed happily as the cool water surrounded me.

The water was a little clearer here, but not as clear as I was used to.

The others joined us and swam around me in a tornado of seals.

I laughed and dived after them, descending towards the ocean floor.

They continued to swim around me as we descended, then stopped, holding me back as we all looked at the shipwreck below. It had been a huge ship, but sat broken in half on the floor now.

I looked at the front of the ship and my eyes widened. A mermaid figurehead with a heart shaped necklace caught my eye.

"Do you know what ship this is?" I asked in a near scream, pushing past them.

The seals spun around me once and then headed back to the surface.

Instead of following them, assuming they just needed to take another breath, I dove deeper and headed to the ship of my nightmares.

The human that the mermaid princess had fallen in love with had seen me and he and his crew had tried to kill me. They'd almost succeeded, too with the help of a mage.

I'd tried to find them later, but had never found their ship.

This explained why.

Who had sunk them, though? That was the million yen question.

I swam to the figurehead and snapped her head off. "How's life as seafoam?" I asked the wood head with a sneer.

I swam inside the captain's cabin and stared at the bones of the prince. I could bring him back to life and make him my servant. I could enslave him for the rest of my life.

The brothers returned, but they couldn't fit their large bodies into the cabin.

"Should I do it?" I asked, turning to look at them.

They all shook their heads.

"You don't even know what I'm suggesting," I said.

They backed out of the doorway and I swam out, assuming they wanted me to follow them.

I did, following them to the storage area. Most of it was

gone, most likely washed away during the storm that sank the ship.

"What are we looking for?" I asked.

The guys zipped around, nudging containers and knocking things over.

"It would be so much easier if you could talk," I complained. I sent a bit of my magic out, making the contents of the sealed boxes visible without opening them.

Conall twirled in a circle, making me giggle at the silly joy he had just shown.

They moved about the boxes and then all of them surrounded one box. They hit it with their flippers and tails.

"I get it," I said, pushing Wolfram aside so I could reach the box. I tapped it with my hand and it floated up. With a shove, it floated out of the ship and headed towards the surface.

I grabbed a corner and waved to the guys as I was pulled along with it.

They swam after me, chasing me while swimming around each other and hitting each other.

Were they racing?

I surfaced with the box and my eyes widened at the humans pointing their guns at me.

"What do we have here?" one of the humans asked.

I dropped a hand down and waved at the brothers to warn them back, and shifted my tentacles to legs.

Since they didn't surface, I assumed that meant they heeded my warning.

"What do you want?" I asked them, leaning on the box like I was weak.

"What's in the box?" the same human who had spoken before asked.

I shrugged. "Not sure. I just pulled it up. I haven't opened it yet."

"Pull it in, boys," the man ordered.

Three humans grabbed a net and prepared to throw it at me. No way.

With a mighty kick, I propelled myself and the box away from them and towards our ship.

Wolfram tossed out a line and I grasped it.

When had they gotten on the ship? I hadn't even heard them jump out of the water.

"Who goes there?" the human captain asked.

"Were you attempting to steal my girl?" Wolfram asked with a scowl. "I don't take kindly to men trying to take my girl."

"What's in that box?" the captain asked.

"None of your concern," Wolfram snapped.

The captain leaned forward. "I think it is my concern. You're in my waters and you're taking my treasure."

"I didn't see you down there getting the box," Wolfram said. "And you don't own these waters."

Phelan and Marrok waited as I used my magic to make the box light, so I could hold it while they pulled me up.

"How are you able to hold that box?" one of the humans asked. "That has to weigh a ton."

"Maybe you're just weak and pathetic," I said and smiled warmly at him.

"I know you," another human yelled.

I looked over at him and my eyes widened. "Shit, he does know me," I whispered to Marrok who held my forearm.

"How?" he asked.

"I sold him a potion a few years back," I said.

"She's a witch," the man yelled.

Marrok and Phelan finally pulled me and the box onto the ship, and Wolfram spun the wheel, steering us away from the humans.

"After them," the captain yelled.

"Wonderful," I muttered. "The humans are chasing us."

"Can you disable their ship without killing them?" Wolfram asked.

I rolled my eyes. "Don't belittle me."

Turning, I held my hand out and sent a few tendrils of my dark magic out to snap their rudder. Their ship continued sailing the direction it had been headed and no matter how hard the captain turned the wheel, he could not get it to change course.

We sailed away, and I waved to the humans.

"Stop taunting them," Marrok said.

"No," I said and smiled at him over my shoulder.

After an hour of sailing, and being certain that we had lost the humans, the guys gathered on the deck around the box.

"So, what is in this box that you guys are so interested in?" I asked. When I'd done the initial scan, I hadn't seen anything that seemed all that special.

"Patience," Wolfram said.

He used a metal bar to open the lid and then hopped into the box.

I started to move closer, but Phelan grabbed me and shook his head. "No, you have to wait."

"Why? I want to look inside, too," I said and stuck my bottom lip out in a pout.

"That's an excellent pout," Conall said.

"Not good enough, though," Wolfram said and hopped back out of the box.

He held a fist-sized wooden box with strange symbols carved into the sides. The symbols looked somewhat familiar, but I couldn't place them.

"What is that?" I asked.

Wolfram hid it behind his back and walked away from me. "You'll find out soon enough."

Phelan and Conall grabbed several other items out of the box, and then took them below deck.

"Okay, you can look inside now," Marrok said and released me.

"Oh, how kind of you to allow me your leftovers," I said and shook my head. Still, I went to the box and shuffled the items around inside.

Nothing remotely worthwhile remained. I sighed and walked to my cabin. "Wake me up when we get somewhere fun."

CHAPTER TWENTY

THE GUYS DIDN'T WAKE ME.

Instead, Conall climbed into bed with me at some point, spooning himself around me.

I woke sweaty, but super comfortable.

"It's too early to be awake," Conall mumbled and pulled me closer.

I cuddled into his chest and placed several light kisses against his neck.

"If you keep doing that, I'll be forced to wake up and deal with this growing issue," he whispered and his grip tightened on me.

I thrust my butt backwards and ground against him. "Wake up, then."

He growled, rolled on top of me, and began kissing me while pressing his erection against my already aching center. He pulled back long enough to pull off my shirt and then began kissing his way around my chest.

I gasped and arched up into him.

He slid a hand beneath my butt and gripped while thrusting against me.

"Too many clothes," I gasped and snapped my fingers, making our clothes disappear.

"Yes," he growled and plunged into me.

I gripped his shoulders, trying not to dig my fingernails in too much, meeting his thrusts with my own.

An orgasm ripped through me, and I screamed Conall's name.

"Yes," he growled and gripped the headboard as he moved faster.

Floating on a cloud of bliss and multiple orgasms, we lay in a sweaty cuddle puddle.

"You good?" he asked, panting behind me.

"Yes. You?"

"Definitely," he whispered and kissed right behind my ear.

"Can we go back to sleep now?" I asked, rolling over so I could lay my head on his chest.

"No, now it is time for food," he said and sat up.

"No," I gasped and reached for him, but he was already out of bed.

He chuckled and asked, "Can you give me some clothes?"

"No. You'll have to come back here and climb into bed with me," I said with a victorious smile.

He threw open the door and walked out. "It's fine. My brothers have seen me naked plenty of times."

I stared out the door and waited.

"What the hell, man? Put on some clothes," Marrok yelled.

I fell off the bed laughing, tangled in the sheets.

Marrok looked inside, scowling, but that quickly changed when he saw my naked body sprawled on the floor. "Are you okay?"

I nodded and wiped at my eyes. "Yeah."

"Breakfast is ready," he said, not bothering to hide the fact that he was ogling my body.

"Like what you see?" I asked with a smirk.

He nodded. "If your stomach wasn't growling so loudly, I'd show you just how much I like what I see."

I licked my lips, crawled on my hands and knees towards him, and looked up from his feet. "I don't think you like what you see at all."

His pants had an obvious bulge as I looked up at him. "Evil temptress," he whispered and spun away.

I laughed and conjured some clothes for myself. I made my way below deck to where the guys were gathered for breakfast. The scent of cooking meat made my stomach growl.

Phelan kissed my cheek as I walked to the table. "Morning, beautiful."

"Morning," I said and sat beside Wolfram.

He kissed my cheek and rested his hand on my leg. "Did you sleep well?"

I nodded. "You?"

He leaned closer and whispered, "I would have slept a lot better if you were with me."

"Maybe you can share my bed tonight," I whispered back.

He slid his hand up my leg, stopping just short of my crotch. "I like that idea."

Marrok set a pan of cooked eggs on the table, Phelan brought out a basket of rolls, and Conall set some fruit before me.

I filled my plate with a bit of everything and ate until I couldn't fit another bite.

"That was delicious," I said.

"What do you usually eat living in your cave?" Conall asked.

"Seafood," I said. "When I go see Hammerhead I usually stop by one of the nearby countries and eat their food."

"That sounds really boring," Wolfram said with a scowl.

I shrugged. "It is what it is."

"Well, that's something we will definitely change while you are with us," Wolfram said.

The thought of being with them for a long period of time was really growing on me. The house their father had given me was definitely a huge step in accomplishing that objective.

"What are you daydreaming about?" Phelan asked from across the table.

"The house your dad gave me," I admitted.

"Our house," Wolfram said.

I scowled. "So, if you decide to leave me, I can't keep it?"

He returned my scowl with one of his own. "We're not going to leave you, Uschi. We love you."

Love. Still...so weird.

"People fall out of love," I whispered.

"No, they don't. You know that," he said. "True love is forever. It transcends time."

"Wolfram, you should stop talking. You're starting to sound romantic," I teased.

He stood and before I could react, had me swept up into his arms. "I'll be as romantic as you want me to be, but I am fairly certain you don't want me to be super mushy and romantic."

"Romantic every now and then is good," I whispered.

He smiled, a true and earnest smile. Then he kissed me. I melted into the kiss, my heart pounding.

These guys made me react so differently than any of my previous flings. Maybe because they weren't flings, but a true relationship that involved love.

"Where are we sailing?" I asked to change the subject and tapped Wolfram's arm to put me down.

He set me down with a small smile. "A surprise."

I gave him my best glare. "This whole trip has been a surprise. I still have no idea what you got out of that box."

"I have to stop at a port on the way to our next destination," Wolfram said. "We'll be there probably a full day, and then we can continue on."

"I do not enjoy secrets."

"Not secrets, surprises," Conall said.

"Same crap," I said. I blew out a breath and headed towards the stairs. "I'm going to go for a swim. Don't worry, I can keep pace with the ship."

"Want some company?" Marrok asked.

"No, but you're a grown man so you can do what you want," I said with a dismissive wave over my shoulder without looking back at them.

I leapt off the ship and shifted as I fell, letting my tentacles out. The cool water rushed up around me and I spun in it, falling deeper into the sea so the sun was a milky blob.

Once I was deep enough, I followed the ship, swimming and spinning around as I enjoyed being back in the ocean. I could live on land, but I loved the ocean too much and it made up too much of my life to not come back often.

Schools of fish veered out of my way, sensing a predator nearby.

I watched a giant turtle swimming, peaceful eyes watching the surroundings, without a care. Sometimes I thought it might be nice to be a turtle.

A pod of dolphins swam near me, but kept their distance. They had a few calves, and I thought they might come attack me, but then a pair of seals dove into the water beside me.

Marrok and Conall.

I smiled at them. "Hello."

They swam, one on each side of me.

The dolphins started to approach, but Marrok showed them his teeth and the dolphins altered their course.

"So fierce," I teased.

I'd never seen it before, hadn't even known it was possible, but Marrok in seal form rolled his eyes at me.

I laughed. "A seal rolling its eyes is probably one of the weirdest things I've seen this year."

He blew bubbles out of his nose.

The water around us changed, the currents shifting, and the temperature dropping quickly.

I spun around, and using my magic, I searched for the source.

I couldn't detect anything.

"That's not good," I whispered.

Conall grabbed my shirt in his teeth and pulled me towards the ship, which was getting away from us.

Something wasn't right. What had caused that?

"Ursula!" Poseidon bellowed.

"Oh, shit," I whispered.

I put Marrok and Conall in a sphere of water and shot them up and out of the water and onto the ship.

A lightning bolt of magic zipped past me, narrowly missing my face.

I spun around and came face to face with Poseidon, his eyes deranged and his hair disheveled.

"Poseidon," I said softly. "You look rather handsome today."

He reached out and grabbed me by the throat, squeezing tight enough to cut off my oxygen supply. "Today, you die, Sea Witch."

I used one of my tentacles to hit him in the crotch.

He released me with a curse.

I swam back, away from him, and gathered my magic. "If you attack me again, I will defend myself. I don't care if you're a god or a human, if you attack me, you lose your status and position."

"You think you're so tough," he scoffed. "You're just a peon.

An insignificant wench who was given too much power by some idiot god when he made you. I don't even know who made you, since no one will fess up to it. They were obviously drunk."

"I was born, not made," I said calmly. He was trying to rile me up. I wouldn't let him.

"And even your parents don't want you," he said with a smug smirk.

I shrugged. "Their loss."

He yelled and tried to stab me with his trident.

"Why are you mad at me?" I asked, dodging his attacks. "I gave you back your wife. I left your waters. What more do you want from me?"

"For you to die," he snarled.

"No can do," I said and clapped my hands together between us. The water shoved him backwards, away from me.

He tumbled head over heels in the water a moment before stopping himself. "I command the seas," he said, his eyes glowing and the water beginning to swirl beneath him.

Oh, crap.

I couldn't look towards the guys and their boat, so I sent some magic in their last known location to push them farther away if they were coming closer.

"You're a pathetic knock off of a god who has gone insane from being too old and too stupid to know better. A true god would never let an insignificant peon like me bother them," I said.

I drew on all of my power, letting my body grow and allowing my dark tendrils surround my body.

"You will die today," Poseidon said. "Your blood will darken the seas and then it will be cleaner for it."

"You make no sense," I said and rolled my eyes. "No wonder Amphitrite ran away from you."

That had been the wrong thing to say.

He bellowed in rage and began shooting electric bolts from his trident at me.

I deflected them with my tendrils, but every time I used one, that tendril disappeared. I couldn't do this forever. I had to go on the offensive.

Poseidon raised his trident, preparing to attack again, but a seal snagged the trident with his teeth and swam away with it.

Poseidon roared.

Four seals swam around behind Poseidon, tossing the trident back and forth to each other.

Poseidon swam after them.

I couldn't follow because the whirlpool Poseidon had created beneath himself was growing and if I moved closer, it would swallow me up.

"Bring it here," I called out to the guys.

They swam far around the whirlpool, and I swam to meet them.

Poseidon beat me, though, and grabbed the seal with the trident, Marrok.

Marrok tossed the trident to Conall, and then bit Poseidon on the shoulder.

Poseidon punched Marrok, and I screamed when Marrok's eyes rolled up into the back of his head.

Wolfram swam to Poseidon, hitting him with his flippers, and then grabbed Marrok and swam away.

If I could get to land, I would be at an advantage against Poseidon. The guys weren't as great at fighting in seal form.

I tried to sense land nearby, but there was nothing close. Everything was too far away. However, the land I did sense told me exactly where we were, and a plan began to form in my mind.

Conall passed the trident to Phelan as I swam as fast as I could.

Why were they so damn far away?

Poseidon raised his hands and the whirlpool began pulling Marrok and Wolfram into its base.

"No," I screamed.

Why was I so useless?

No, I wasn't. I could defeat him. I just had to get the guys away first.

They were sea creatures and I prayed this crazy plan would work.

I created new tendrils and snagged Wolfram and Marrok. I couldn't pull them out of the whirlpool, but I could hold them where they were.

"Conall. Phelan. Give him his trident and come here," I ordered them.

They wanted to argue, I could see it in them, but Phelan tossed the trident away, in the opposite direction so Poseidon had to swim after it.

Conall and Phelan swam to me. I wrapped them in tendrils, kissed each of their noses, slid my upper arm cuff off and put it on Conall's fin, and then sent them so they were floating beside their brothers.

Once they were all touching, I whispered, "Sealed."

The brothers' eyes widened as the magic activated and began to teleport them away.

"I love you," I whispered.

Poseidon yelled and swam towards the brothers. I swam into his path to keep him from getting closer to them, and he stabbed me in the side with his trident.

CHAPTER TWENTY-ONE

I pushed away from Poseidon, clutching at my wound. My blood spilled out into the sea.

"You sent them away?" Poseidon asked, looking down at the whirlpool where the guys had just been. "Why?"

"To protect them," I said. "When you love someone, you protect them."

"You aren't capable of love," he snarled.

I shrugged. "I have no interest in arguing that point with you." Using some magic, I stopped my wound from bleeding. I couldn't heal it, but I could at least keep from bleeding out while we fought.

"It's a shame," he whispered. "I had hoped for them to witness your death."

"Then why try to kill them?" I asked with a scoff.

"Today, your life ends," he said. His tone was cold, flat, and matter-of-factly. "Your darkness has tainted my seas far too long."

"You do not own all of the seas," I said. "There are other gods."

"There are no gods who can defeat me," Poseidon said, his

eyes glowing again.

"Is that a challenge?" Kanaloa asked as he swam to me.

I smirked as Poseidon's eyes widened.

Kanaloa, god of the Underworld, Ruler of the Ocean, and Teacher of Magic was as handsome as he was powerful. He also was represented by squid and octopus, which I found out when he saw me and thought I was created by another god as a present for him. It took me a week to convince him I was not.

"Kanaloa," I said and bowed.

"It has been too long," Kanaloa said.

I smiled. "I shall try to visit more often."

He looked over at Poseidon. "Are the Greeks becoming defective?"

"This one has," I said.

"This fight is not your concern. It is between me and Ursula," Poseidon said and pointed his trident at me.

Kanaloa glared at Poseidon's trident. "That weapon is not fitting for such a pathetic creature as yourself."

Poseidon's eyes narrowed. "Excuse me?"

"You are in my waters—" Kanaloa began, but Poseidon cut him off.

"I am the God of the Sea! All seas," Poseidon snapped, his eyes wide and bloodshot.

I glanced over at Kanaloa, finding his eyes dark and brows furrowed. I knew from personal experience that he hated being interrupted when speaking.

I swam back, away from both of the gods, preparing to flee as far and as fast as I could if things got too volatile. Fights between gods often became out of control.

"You are nothing more than a spoiled ignorant man-child," Kanaloa said. "I've grown tired of your existence. Today, I will wipe your stain from this planet."

Oh, snap. It was about to go down.

Poseidon raised his trident, making the whirlpool swirl faster and move towards Kanaloa.

Kanaloa rolled his eyes, waved his hand, and the whirlpool disappeared. "Child," he spat. He held out his hand and a beautiful spear appeared in it. He twirled it, roared, and then darted forward, thrusting his spear at Poseidon.

Poseidon spun, narrowly avoiding the spear. He attempted to stab Kanaloa, but Kanaloa knocked the trident away.

The two battled so quickly that the water began to churn, and I was certain there were waves on the surface.

"The ship," I gasped. I swam as fast as I could, shooting up out of the water and landed on the deck of the ship.

As I'd thought, the waves were strong, and I had to quickly secure the masts and steer the ship away from the gods' battle.

Normal means were not enough. I had to use magic to escape the massive swells and prevent the ship from sinking.

I made it to a decent sized island, wrapped the ship in a magic bubble, and made it float several feet onto the island. Carefully, I set it down on the land, cringing as the wood creaked.

Fully set down, I popped an invisibility shell over it, just in case any humans happened by.

The ship safe, I prepared to dive back into the water and head back towards the battle. One look at the ocean and I decided that was a very bad idea.

"What did you do this time, Ursula?" Kane, Father of Living Creatures and companion of Kanaloa asked as he floated above the water before me.

"It wasn't me this time. The Greek God insulted Kanaloa," I said.

Kane's eyes hardened. "Which one?"

"Poseidon, God of the Sea," I said.

Kane scoffed. "God. Pft."

"I was going to go back and help fight, but—"

"You stay here, Leilani. I'll go and help Kanaloa," he said.

Leilani, Heavenly Flower. It had been a very long time since I'd been called that.

I bowed. "Yes, Kane."

He gave me a look and then disappeared.

I sat on the beach and watched the swells.

What were the guys doing right now? How mad were they?

Now, I almost regretted sending them away. Had I known Kanaloa would show up, I wouldn't have done it.

Okay, that wasn't true. I still would have. Seeing Marrok and Wolfram headed down the whirlpool had terrified me.

How mad at me were they? When I returned to them, would they end our relationship?

I didn't think so, but then again I wasn't very familiar with relationships yet.

"What are you doing?" Muirin asked.

I turned around, eyes wide. "Muirin? What are you doing here? This isn't your territory."

"I have four distraught sons who seem to think you're in a battle against a Greek God." He looked around. "Yet, I've found you lounging on a beach. I thought you said you wouldn't run from them? You promised to give them a chance."

"I—"

He held up his hand. "No, I won't hear any lies or excuses from you. I will bring you back to my sons and—"

"I can't go back yet. Poseidon is fighting the Hawaiians and it is my fault. I would have gone to intercept, but their leader told me to stay here," I said quickly, interrupting him.

Muirin looked out over the sea, saw the thrashing waves, the dark sky with abnormal lightning, and sighed. "What do you want to do?" he asked.

"I just need to see how things pan out here. The boys were

almost sucked into a whirlpool that Poseidon had created. I panicked and sent them to you to keep them safe. If they come back now and Poseidon attacks again, they could die this time. Let me finish this with Poseidon first."

"They could help you. They are fighters," he said.

"Please," I begged.

He looked skyward and grumbled something. Then, he held out the arm cuff he had given me before. "Say, 'deal' and a portal will open that the boys can step through to come to you."

I stood and hugged him. "Thank you."

"They're going to kill me," he whispered. He plucked a strand of hair from my head.

"What the barnacles are you doing?" I asked and rubbed my head.

"This will let me know if you are in danger or not," he said.

I eyed my hair, unsure how he could do that, but then remembered he was a god. "Okay."

"This is the only way that they'll agree to stay back," he said. "Even with this they may want to come after you."

"I'll try to be quick."

He shook his head and disappeared.

"Why are you bringing other gods to my territory?" Hina, Goddess of the Moon asked.

I bowed to her. "I'm sorry. I didn't bring him. He teleported to me. He won't be coming back, though."

"Why are you here, Leilani?" she asked. "The last time you were here you said you were going on a soul search."

"Lots has happened since then," I whispered sadly.

"Who is causing all this chaos? My beautiful moon cannot be seen by any of the islands."

"A Greek God is fighting Kane and Kanaloa," I said. "Could you take me to their fight so I can see what is going on?"

"I'm not a transportation service," she said and narrowed her eyes at me.

"I want to watch as they kill him," I said. "Don't you want to see that, too?"

She smiled. "You know me too well. Alright, come touch my arm and I'll take you."

I loved her accent so much. I would sit and listen to her talk for days on end if I could. I put two fingertips against her arm and she teleported us over the ocean where a massive whirlpool swirled around the three gods as they battled.

Poseidon was bleeding from many wounds and breathing heavily. His eyes were wide and wild—he looked like a demon.

"He's definitely not winning," Hina whispered.

Kanaloa thrust his spear at Poseidon.

Lightning flashed overhead, and then Zeus stood between the three gods, a lightning bolt in his hand.

"Uh oh," I whispered.

"Who is that?" Hina asked.

"Leader of the Greek Pantheon," I said.

Zeus looked up at me. "What is the meaning of this?"

"He attacked me. Kanaloa showed up because this is his territory and Poseidon insulted him. Poseidon is crazed, Zeus. He needs to be put down," I said.

Zeus narrowed his eyes. "There are those who need to be put down, but he is not one of them."

Kanaloa snapped, "Do not threaten our friend while we are standing right in front of you."

"You know he's insane. You were planning to open Tartarus and throw him in there," I said to Zeus.

He scowled. "Who told you that?"

"A worried Goddess," I said. I may not have liked Ceto much, but I wouldn't out her to Zeus.

"Zeus, step aside and let me finish this," Poseidon said, his breathing ragged.

"You're cut up and can barely stand," Zeus said. "You won't win this battle."

Poseidon bellowed and tried to stab Zeus with his trident.

Zeus's eyes flew open, and he dodged out of the way. Poseidon tried again to stab Zeus, the crazed look growing, and the god I had known years ago was barely recognizable.

Zeus's eyes narrowed, and he plunged a lightning bolt into Poseidon's chest.

I gasped, and Hina muttered something that sounded like a prayer.

Poseidon staggered backwards, staring at the lightning bolt sizzling in his chest.

Zeus bore down on him. "You tried to kill me. Your punishment shall be death."

Poseidon continued to stare at the lightning bolt, but when Zeus was within arm's length, he thrust his trident into Zeus's stomach, angled upwards so that it pierced his heart. "You go with me then, brother."

Holy nectar.

"Hades!" I screamed as loud as I could, sending the scream as a prayer and a plea.

Hades appeared in front of me. "What?"

I pointed at his brothers.

He looked down and instead of being upset, he smiled. "About time. I wondered how long it was before they died."

"Will you take them out of our territory?" Kane asked.

Hades bowed. "I apologize for their intrusion, and mine. I will take them away and you will never hear from them again."

Kanaloa looked irritated, but he nodded.

Hades looked back to me. "Next week, I will visit you to discuss what happened today."

I nodded. "Okay."

Hades set a hand on each of his brothers, both barely breathing. "You're going to enjoy the Underworld. I've got your places all picked out and waiting for you."

His terrifying and evil laugh was the last thing we heard before he teleported.

"Those Greeks are so screwed up," Hina said.

"You don't know the half of it," I whispered.

I continued to stare down at the place the Greek Gods had just been. Never in my life had I expected to see Zeus and Poseidon killed, and especially not by each other.

"You going to be around for a while?" Kanaloa asked.

I shrugged. "I was on a vacation with my boyfriends. Poseidon sent some of his sons after us, and then came after us when his son failed. I don't know where they were headed, but we were sailing towards your islands. They wouldn't tell me what the plan was."

"Where are they?" Hina asked.

"I sent them away when Poseidon tried to kill them," I said.

"Well, you better bring them back before they want to skin you, Leilani," Kanaloa said with a smirk.

He was probably right.

CHAPTER TWENTY-TWO

Kanaloa set the ship back in the water, dropping the anchor so it wouldn't float away while I opened the portal.

I'd expected the gods to leave now that the Greeks were gone, but they stood together on the island, whispering to each other.

I took a deep breath and rubbed the arm cuff. "Deal," I said.

A swirling green portal opened beside me and immediately, four men walked through, swords drawn.

Kanaloa and Kane tensed.

"It's okay," I told my guys. "I'm safe. The Greeks are gone and these three are friends."

The boys dropped their swords and converged on me. I stood within their circle, feeling emotions swelling within me and threatening to break free.

"Don't you ever do that again," Wolfram growled into my ear.

"Sorry not sorry," I whispered. "I couldn't let you die."

"Where's Poseidon?" Conall asked. "Did they kill him?"

All four turned to look at the Hawaiian gods.

"Almost, but no they did not. Let me introduce you first," I said. I walked to the Hawaiians, the guys right behind me. "Kane, Kanaloa, and Hina, gods of the Hawaiians and rulers of this territory, please meet my boyfriends. Wolfram, Conall, Marrok, and Phelan." As I said their names, the guys shook hands with Kanaloa and Kane, and then bowed to Hina.

"Thank you for protecting Uschi," Wolfram said and bowed to them. The three others bowed as well.

"Uschi?" Kanaloa asked.

"That's the name I go by now," I explained with a smile.

He smiled. "I like it."

"What were you sailing to in our territory?" Hina asked.

Wolfram glanced at me and then turned back to Hina. "It's a surprise. May I come closer to keep Uschi from hearing?"

Hina's face lit up. She loved secrets. "Yes, come closer."

Wolfram walked to her and whispered in her ear.

Her eyes widened and then began to shine as she smiled. "That is a wonderful surprise."

I sighed and looked up at the sky. "I hate surprises."

"May we help with this surprise?" Kanaloa asked.

I dipped my chin and gaped at him. "What?"

Wolfram smiled. "That would be great."

"One week?" Hina asked.

"Three days?" Wolfram asked back.

Kanaloa laughed. "Sure of yourself, are you?"

Wolfram shrugged. "There are only two possible outcomes."

Hina smiled. "Three days is fine."

"Can I take some coconuts from the island for our ship?" I asked.

Kane nodded. "Take whatever you need from this island. It is uninhabited."

Phelan and Marrok joined me as I walked around the small island, taking coconuts and a few other items.

Once the ship was stocked, I bowed to the Hawaiians and thanked them for their help again.

They waved as we set sail and then disappeared.

"So, what happened?" Phelan asked.

"Shortly after I sent you guys back to your dad, Kanaloa showed up. Poseidon insulted him, so they started fighting. I saved the ship and was going to return to the fight, but the seas were out of control due to two sea gods fighting and Kane told me to stay while he went to help. Then Hina showed up and she teleported us over the battle. Poseidon was losing against Kanaloa and Kane. Then Zeus appeared and threatened me. The Hawaiians didn't like that. But in his crazed state Poseidon started attacking Zeus. Zeus stabbed a lightning bolt into Poseidon's chest, and then Poseidon stuck his trident into Zeus. I called on Hades and he took his dying brothers to the Underworld. Then, I opened the portal for you guys," I said.

"Poseidon and Zeus are dead?" Wolfram asked, eyes wide.

I nodded.

"Are they dead dead? Or are they going to come back?" Conall asked.

"Hades said he had their places picked out in the Underworld and he seemed rather pleased that his brothers were dying. I don't think he'll let them out of the Underworld. At least, not any time soon," I said. Knowing that family, someone would eventually free the two gods, but I hoped that I was dead long before that happened.

"Thank you for saving the ship and our cargo," Wolfram said. "I would have been pretty irritated to have lost the treasure we'd just found."

The clouds opened and the moon shone down upon us as the first rays of sunlight began to peek on the horizon.

"This was not how I saw my vacation with you going," I admitted.

The guys laughed.

"This was not what we'd planned either," Conall said.

"I'm still mad that you sent us away," Marrok said with arms folded across his chest.

"I thought you were going to die. What would you have done if you'd seen me headed into the whirlpool and you couldn't bring me out of it? You would have teleported me to safety, too."

He sighed and dropped his arms. "Yeah, you're right."

I smiled. "I'm always right."

Phelan steered the ship, his eyes focused ahead.

"Where are we going?" I asked. "Don't I at least get a hint?"

"Somewhere beautiful," Conall said.

That was so not helpful.

"Can you tell me how long until we're there?" I asked.

Wolfram pulled me into a hug and then tied a blindfold around my eyes. "In just a few minutes. Until then, you have to keep the blindfold on."

I grumbled, but allowed it.

"I'm fairly certain you will really enjoy our surprise," Marrok said.

"Fairly certain?" I asked.

"Well, you are a bit unpredictable at times," he said and chuckled.

I plopped down and folded my arms over my chest. "Well, I'll behave until we get there. You guys are clearly excited about this and have spent time planning it. So, I won't ruin it for you."

My statement was greeted by silence.

"I am reasonable most of the time," I muttered.

Someone sat down beside me and kissed my cheek. I inhaled. Conall.

"You're amazing," Conall whispered.

"I wouldn't go that far," I mumbled.

His lips pressed against my throat, and I tilted my head to give him better access.

"You're amazing. Beautiful. Powerful."

Each word was punctuated with a kiss to my neck.

"Sexy. Intelligent. Perfect."

A hand pressed on my thigh and then slid up, stopping much too low for my liking.

"You're also infuriating and have to stop trying to face things alone. We're a team now and you have to work with us," he whispered in my ear, his fingers tapping on the inside of my upper thigh.

"I can definitely work with you," I said breathily.

"Conall," Phelan snapped.

Conall kissed my cheek and then moved away from me.

"Cock blocker," I yelled at Phelan.

Four laughs echoed around me.

Sometime later, the anchor chains rustled and then the ship lurched to a stop.

Warm arms picked me up.

"It's dinner time," Marrok said as he carried me.

"We're not there yet?" I asked.

"No, we have to stay the night, actually. Then, we'll be there," he said.

I huffed. "Do I have to keep the blindfold on all night?"

"Yes," Marrok said.

He set me down on the bench at the table, and then removed the blindfold.

I rubbed my eyes as they adjusted to the light in the dining area, even as dim as it was, it was brighter than the blindfold had been. "I thought you said I had to keep it on?"

Wolfram smiled. "You can have it off while we're down here and eating. Then it goes back on."

I didn't waste the time I'd been given and ate the food

quickly. I didn't want them feeding me blindfolded because I didn't trust them not to feed me something gross for their amusement.

They teased each other and pushed and shoved at each other a bit while eating. I found myself enthralled by their brotherly love and affection. I had seen it many times before, but seeing it now for some reason made me even more determined to keep them with me.

When the last one had eaten his fill, the blindfold was put back on.

"Aren't we going to sleep? Why do I have to be blindfolded to sleep?" I asked.

Wolfram walked in front of me with my hands on his shoulders. Marrok walked behind me, ready to adjust my course if I needed it.

"We didn't say we were sleeping yet," Wolfram said.

A door opened, and then someone picked me up and laid me down on a bed.

I sighed as the soft mattress and blankets gave a bit beneath me, cushioning me.

Then my pants were removed, and someone removed my shirt.

Marrok groaned. "I keep forgetting that she doesn't wear undergarments."

I chuckled. "So, this is what you meant about not sleeping yet."

One hand slid between my legs, rubbing me and making me moan, while a pair of hands stroked my breasts and pinched my nipples gently.

Another pair of hands gripped my butt, lifted, and then someone was pushing inside of me.

I gasped, my senses on overload as so many hands worked to pleasure me.

A mouth crashed into mine at the same time that two mouths sucked on my nipples.

I moaned into the mouth kissing me, which I was fairly certain was Conall, and arched my hips as the person sliding in and out of me brought me closer to the precipice of orgasm.

The hand working my clit hadn't stopped, and I wanted to kiss them. Then again, maybe I was.

The orgasm crashed over me and I screamed, but the sound was muffled by the kiss.

That person pulled out of me and another replaced them, this one a bit larger.

I wanted to see them, to see what they were doing to me with their hands and mouths, but it was also almost better not to see it and only feel and hear it.

The person kissing me moved to nibbling on my neck and I gasped in pleasure.

The rhythm increased all around and another orgasm tore a scream from my throat.

I lost count of the number of orgasms, the number of times they switched off who was inside of me, and lost myself to the bliss.

When all of them had found their release, I lay in a boneless puddle of ecstasy. Had I been a feline, I would have purred.

It took me approximately two minutes to fall into a deep sleep, the first time I'd fallen asleep that quickly without magical or medicinal means in a decade.

Not even my anxiety over what tomorrow would bring kept me from falling into a deep and undisturbed sleep.

CHAPTER TWENTY-THREE

"Uschi, it's time to wake up," Phelan whispered in my ear.

I pulled him closer. "More sleep."

He lay on my chest and chuckled. "No, you have to get up. It's time."

Time?

Oh, right. Their surprise.

I sat up and he helped me stand off the bed. Then, I used my magic to create new clothes for myself. "Are these appropriate?" I asked.

"Yes," he said and kissed my cheek. "I'm going to pick you up."

He lifted me into his arms and carried me out of my cabin. The cold air hit me and I shivered a moment, craving the warm bed I'd just been pulled from.

He jumped down and a few more hands steadied us.

No one spoke.

The little boat we were in moved, and Phelan sat with me in his lap.

The boat went over a few small waves, and water crashed against the beach.

The boat lurched as it hit land. Phelan stood with me and jumped from the boat, cool ocean water spraying up around us as he landed.

He splashed through the water, towards the shore, I assumed. A bit later, he set my feet down while keeping an arm around my waist to steady me. Sure I was stable, he released me and stepped away.

"You can remove your blindfold now," Wolfram said.

I raised my hands, but hesitated. This was it. Once I took this off I would see whatever their surprise was. If I didn't react how they wanted me to, I would upset them.

"Uschi," all four said.

I removed the blindfold, my eyes widened, and a gasp escaped.

The four selkie males wore suits, stood before the famous lava waterfall. A waterfall that when the sun hit it at a specific time of morning made the water look like lava.

They stood before it and it was the most beautiful thing I had seen.

As one, they dropped to one knee and Wolfram held out a gorgeous ring.

"Uschi, we have gone through a lot of trials, tribulations, and quests," Marrok said.

"We've hurt you, saved you, and fallen in love with you," Phelan said.

"You've brought us adventure, fun, and something that we didn't even know we were missing," Conall said.

"Will you marry us?" Wolfram asked.

Tears had started flowing when Marrok had finished his statement, and now they were flowing in earnest.

"Yes," I said and walked to them and stopped before the four men who had stolen my heart. "Yes, I will marry you."

They stood.

Wolfram slid the ring onto my finger and I laughed loudly when I saw it. It was the engagement ring that Triton's daughter had picked out, thinking the prince was going to ask her to marry him.

I had no idea how the ship had made it all the way to the Pacific, but I was not complaining.

"It's perfect," I said and looked up at them.

They each took a turn kissing me, and then we turned and watched the lava waterfall.

"I love you," Wolfram whispered in my ear.

I leaned my head against his shoulder. "I love you, too." I turned and looked at the others. "All of you."

Once the sun rose fully, we boarded the ship and set sail again.

"Now where are we going?" I asked, still examining my new ring. There was something about it, something magical. "Did you have someone charm this?"

"Dad said he added something special to the ring and swore it wasn't anything bad," Marrok said. "Is it bad?"

I shrugged. "I can't tell what it is. It doesn't feel bad. Plus, Muirin and I get along pretty well, and he loves you guys, so I don't think he would put a spell to kill me or anything on it."

"He better not," Wolfram growled.

I sat on the railing before the wheel and switched between watching the water and staring at my ring.

Engaged. I was engaged.

I never would have imagined it.

Okay, I had imagined it, but I never thought it would actually happen.

"Where are we going to get married?" I asked. "Humans don't marry more than one husband to a wife." They'd marry seventy women to one man, but not more than one man to a woman. Sexist.

"We know of a place," Wolfram said with a small smirk.

"You guys thought of everything, didn't you?" I asked.

"Well, we couldn't decide what we would do if you said no," Marrok said and laughed.

"We were torn between begging, crying, and stalking," Phelan said.

I threw my head back as I laughed and then had to hop down from the railing to hold my stomach as the laughter began to hurt my stomach.

"I appreciate your candid honesty with me," I said as I wiped the tears of laughter from my face.

"We decided that, with you, we are to be completely honest, even if it is embarrassing or dangerous," Conall said.

"Are you guys going to be okay sharing a house with zombies?" I asked. "Because they're pretty much non-negotiable."

"We would never try to separate you from Blackleg and his crew," Wolfram said.

"Are you fine with being so close to your dad?" I asked.

They nodded.

"We had a rocky start with our dad, but he's been trying hard to make it up to us. I think this is one of his ways to make reparations," Marrok said.

"He really is a good god," I said. "And you know I mean that when I say it."

"Just how did you get to know so many gods?" Wolfram asked.

"I did a lot of traveling in my early adulthood. My power and type of magic draws the attention of gods, especially if I'm in their territory for more than a couple of days," I said. "Sometimes the experiences were good. Sometimes...well, let's just say I had to work out some trust issues with many of them to begin with."

"Why didn't you just go back to the Aztecs when all that stuff happened with Triton?" Wolfram asked. "They seemed fond of you. Or even the Hawaiians? It doesn't seem like you were short on options."

"I wanted a place of my own. Not one given to me by gods who might hold it over my head in the future. I could have gone to their territory, but the Aztecs and Hawaiians aren't as hands off as the Greeks."

"And you hate the hot areas," Phelan added.

I laughed. "Yes. There is that, too."

"Would you be okay with Dad getting Blackleg and his crew and moving all your stuff to your new house while we are still traveling?" Wolfram asked.

I didn't really like other people touching my things, but I supposed in this instance, that it would be okay. I nodded. "Be sure he brings Blackleg's shark."

"Already noted," Muirin's voice said.

I looked around for him, but didn't find him anywhere.

Wolfram held up a bowl of water and I saw Muirin in the reflection.

"Please, let Blackleg do the packing. He knows how I like things sorted," I said loud enough for him to hear.

"Yes, Daughter," he said.

I blinked at him. Daughter? I'd never even been called that before.

"Thanks, Dad," Wolfram said and dumped the water out, ending the communication.

"Where are we going?" I asked.

"To visit friends," Wolfram said.

"Friends? My friends or yours?" I asked.

"Yours," he said.

"Who could you possibly be going to see that is a friend of mine?" I asked with a scowl.

"You'll have to wait to find out," Marrok said.

"I hate waiting," I said in a super whiny voice.

There was no sympathy to be had from the four men around me.

"Torture," I said and lay on my back on the deck. "Pure torture."

"You didn't seem to mind the torture last night," Conall said.

I smiled. "That does not constitute torture."

"Oh, what is it then?" Marrok asked.

"That was pure ecstasy," I said. "The best gift any girl could be given."

They didn't laugh like I thought they would, so I opened my eyes. They were all smiling smugly. I closed my eyes again. They could be smug. They deserved to be smug. Last night had been...magical. Even better than being with a god. Perhaps because technically, I'd been with two gods. Or four half gods.

Another day of sailing, and then we made it to the abandoned island we'd talked to the Hawaiians on.

"Here?" I asked.

The guys loaded a bunch of boxes onto a small boat, ignoring me and my questions.

I stood with my arms folded across my chest, watching them.

What were in the boxes? Why were they loading them to take to the islands? Were the Hawaiians asking for payment for letting us travel through their seas?

They didn't usually ask for payment of any kind.

"Come on, Uschi," Wolfram called.

I looked over and realized they'd all boarded the boat when

I had spaced out. I used my magic to send the boat away, and then dove into the water, reveling in the feel of the salty water on my skin, and swam to shore beneath the surface. At the shore, I walked out and wrung out my hair.

The guys didn't even lecture me about doing that.

They just went about unloading the boat and stacking the boxes.

"I guess I'll just sit over here," I said.

No one responded.

I sat in the surf and let the water lap over me.

"What are you doing in the water?" Hina asked me.

I cracked open an eye. "They were busy and didn't need me, so I am here."

"You need to wash," she said and her eyes widened with urgency. She snapped her fingers and we teleported to a stone cave with a waterfall. She shoved me beneath the waterfall, made my clothes disappear, and then grabbed some flowers and squirted them into my hair.

"Why are you washing me?" I asked.

She scrubbed my hair vigorously. "You're getting married, Leilani. You want to get married dirty?"

"Married?" I gasped.

"Didn't they ask you?" she asked, stepping back with a scowl.

"They asked me to marry them, but we didn't set a date. I didn't know they were going to have the ceremony so soon," I said.

"Which dress?" Persephone asked.

I turned and gaped at the Goddess of Spring standing behind Hina. "What are you doing here?"

"Which dress?" she asked again and waved at a rack of wedding dresses.

"There are some from each of the pantheons you are friends with," Persephone said. "And a couple I designed."

All of the dresses were gorgeous. Some were pure white. Some were black. Some were white with designs.

The one that caught my eye was the black one with white flames.

"This one," I whispered.

Persephone conjured a stool and pointed. "Sit, so I can work on your hair."

I obeyed and it wasn't long before the goddesses had my hair brushed and styled and added several flowers to it.

They helped me into the dress, and Hina created a mirror for me to see.

I didn't look like myself. I didn't look like the hideous creature who had fought against Triton. The sea witch who was accused of killing a mermaid.

I looked like a goddess.

"Stunning," Muirin said.

We all turned.

"What are you doing in here?" Hina asked.

"I'm her father. I'll be walking her down the aisle," he said.

I gaped at him. "What?"

"Unless you have another father-figure you would prefer?" he asked.

I shook my head. "You're the first one to ever call me their daughter."

He scowled. "Well, that is their loss."

"She is ready," Hina said. "Are preparations outside ready?"

He nodded and held out his hand to me. "It is time."

"I'm really doing this? I'm getting married," I whispered.

He smiled. "You are. You are getting married to four wonderful men who care about you very much and are deeply in love with you."

"I'm not getting cold feet," I explained. "I'm just so shocked that I'm getting married. Me."

"You deserve love," Persephone said. "Everyone deserves love."

"They are the lucky ones," Hina said. "Remember that."

I smiled and then hugged them each.

Muirin took my hand and placed it on his arm. Then he teleported us into a huge building with pews on each side and a stage at the front where my four men stood, wearing suits.

In the center of the stage stood Hera, Kane, Huitzilopochtli, and Odin.

The pews were filled with gods, goddesses, and many others I had known over the years, including Hammerhead and Lansa. The most surprisingly was Blackleg just to the side of the front with his shark in a floating water bubble beside him. On his other side was Crusty and Barny in a floating water bubble as well. Blackleg smiled and shook the flower bouquet he was holding. Was he my bridesmaid?

"They're all here for you," Muirin whispered to me. "We invited them, but told them only to come if they were going to behave, and that anyone who tried to hurt you would be killed without mercy."

"If I start crying now, my makeup will be ruined," I whispered.

Muirin patted my hand and led me down the aisle.

Muirin released me and took a seat in the front row beside a woman I didn't even need to ask to know who she was. Conall's mother. She was beautiful, and I could see why Muirin would have picked her.

"Today, we are joined in peace," Odin said.

"Several pantheons who normally fight, but found a single thing that unites us," Kane said.

"Today, we join these five as one," Hera said. "We, the

leaders of our pantheons, bless this marriage and bless these people."

"Marrok, Phelan, Wolfram, and Conall. Do you four take Uschi to be your other half, your mate, your queen? To have no other beside her?" Hera asked.

"Yes," they said at the same time.

"Do you, Uschi, take these four as your mates, your kings, your other pieces? To have no others beside them?" Hera asked.

"Yes," I said.

"You are hereby married, blessed of the gods," Odin said and raised his hands.

Thunder shook the building and everyone cheered.

EPILOGUE

A BEAUTIFUL NECKLACE CAUGHT MY EYE AS WE WALKED BY a jewelry store window. I stopped so abruptly that Marrok, who'd been walking behind me, ran into me.

My four mates looked at the display with varying expressions as I glanced at their reflections in the glass.

"That's a beautiful necklace, isn't it, Uschi?" Conall asked.

"It is beautiful. It would go so well with my new dress," I said, turning to smile at them.

"Phelan, you should buy Uschi that necklace," Marrok said.

Phelan scowled. "Why me?"

Conall smirked. "Remember that time you betrayed Uschi and—"

Phelan cut him off with a sigh, grabbed my hand, and tugged me into the store. "Come on, let's get you that necklace."

"You don't have to," I said, but didn't hide my huge smile.

He ran his thumb across my lower lip. "To see you smile like this, I'll buy you the moon."

Carrying my new necklace in its bag, I walked down the streets of Rome, the guys behind me.

Dust picked up, making me cough.

"Phelan, get Uschi water," Wolfram said and then wiped dust from my face.

"What? There are—"

"Remember that time Uschi was tortured because—" Marrok started.

Phelan sighed. "I'm going."

Once he was out of earshot, I asked, "How long are you guys going to use that against him?"

I'd already forgiven the little jerk.

"Until he dies," Conall said and bent to kiss me. "He has a lot of atoning to do for the pain he caused you."

Phelan handed me a cup of water. "You need anything else?" he asked.

I drank the cup and smiled. "I'm fine."

He took the cup back to the well and then caught up to us as we continued on.

As we headed out of the city, a portal opened in front of us and Muirin stepped out, glaring at me. "You need to deal with your pets."

I laughed. "What happened this time?" For some reason, my pets, Blackleg, and his pirates, liked causing trouble for Muirin.

He reached a hand out for me, but four other hands slapped his away. Muirin glared at his sons, but stepped back through the portal and waited for us to follow.

I stepped through first and my jaw dropped. Pieces of paper were scattered everywhere.

"Barny! Crusty!" I yelled, summoning my pet dog fish.

They swam inside of water orbs that floated in the air. Moving as fast as they could, they circled me.

"What have I told you about paper? You know not to ruin paper," I scolded them.

They spun in a circle inside their orbs.

"They said they're sorry," I told Muirin. The dog fish floated away, playing chase with each other.

"Why do they keep coming here? You have your own house," Muirin grumbled.

"You're the one who made an open portal between our houses," I reminded him.

He looked at my rapidly growing stomach. "That was a necessary precaution."

I rested my hand on my stomach and felt the tiny, fast heart-beats. My entire life I had been told I was infertile. Yet, through some miracle, I had become pregnant right after our wedding.

There had been several fertility goddesses in attendance at the wedding, and all of them were likely culprits. Perhaps they had all used their powers, which would definitely explain the situation at hand.

Wolfram set his hand on my stomach and smiled at me. "Soon, we'll meet our little miracle."

I bit my lip and Muirin folded his arms over his chest.

"Uschi," he said.

I sighed. "Muirin, I wanted to surprise them."

He shook his head. "They should know, so they can prepare better."

"What's he talking about?" Wolfram asked.

All four gathered in front to glare at me.

I sighed and walked away, waving for them to follow.

We stepped through the portal Muirin had created that went from his living room to mine. Walking down the hallway, I stopped at what they all thought was the end, a solid wall.

Waving my hand, the illusion disappeared and the closed door was revealed.

"What's this?" Phelan asked.

"The nursery," I said, turned the knob, and pushed the door open.

They filed in, with me last.

Silence.

The nursery was larger than the living room, but that was necessary to fit the four cribs and four changing tables.

"Surprise," I said. "We're having quadruplets."

My mates spun around, and I was peppered with kisses and hugs all over my face, neck, and stomach.

Tears built, and I sniffled, trying to hold them back. I'd never thought this could be my future. That I would be surrounded with so much love.

Wolfram kissed away my tears. "We love you."

I smiled. "I love you, too."

"Quadruplets!" Conall yelled and ran around the room. "We have so much more to do. We need more names."

"More clothes. More blankets," Phelan said. He disappeared and then returned with a notebook in his hand with several notes already jotted down.

"Your lives are about to get a whole lot more crazy," Muirin said, smiling and unable to hide his excitement.

I laughed. "When isn't my life, crazy?"

Crazy it may be, but this was the perfect crazy for me. Me and my four mates would do everything in our powers to give our children the best lives possible.

And this time, I wouldn't involve myself with garbage hoarding princesses.

CONNECT WITH CATHERINE BANKS

I really appreciate you reading my book! I hope you enjoyed it.

Please consider leaving a review at your favorite site.

Here are some ways to connect with me:

www.catherinebanks.com

Follow me on BookBub: https://www.bookbub.com/authors/catherine-banks

Join my newsletter for deals and snippets: http://catbanks.co/newsletter

Purchase items handmade by Catherine: http://Etsy.com/shop/TurboKittenInd

ACKNOWLEDGMENTS

Thank you to Jenica for being my go to person for discussing this book and volunteering to be a guinea pig to read it first. Being able to bounce ideas off of you was a huge help. You are amazing, lovely, and I'm so lucky to have you in my life. And, you can all thank her for the sequels to come for this book.

Thank you to my beta readers and assistants, Courtney, Lea, and Michelle. You guys rock and I love all your feedback and help finding errors I missed.

A huge thanks to my editor, Pauline, who saved me and ensured I was able to meet my deadline. You are the best.

Jennifer Munswami, thank you for creating this gorgeous cover. I cannot wait to work on the rest of the series.

As always, thank you to my amazing husband (who won't even read this, but that's okay). Your support means everything to me. Thank you for creating my symbols and chapter headers. Formatting is always better when you help me. You're the love of my life and I look forward to spending the rest of my years with you.

MORE FROM CATHERINE BANKS

Calvin's Alien Adventure

Pirate Princess Trilogy
Pirate Princess
Princess Triumvirate
Pirate Queen*

Little Death Bringer Duet
Mercenary
Protector
Little Death Bringer, The Official Coloring Book

Her Royal Harem Series
Royally Entangled
Royally Exposed
Royally Elected
Royally Enraged
Her Royal Harem, The Complete Series
The Demon's Fair
Her Royal Harem, The Coloring Book

Zodiac Shifters Paranormal Romance Series
Centaur's Prize
Tiger Tears
Lion About

The Lioness's Harem Trilogy
Lonely Lioness
Leery Lioness*

Anderelle: Minloa Trilogy
Queen of the Stars
Empress of the Galaxy
Goddess of the Universe*

Bonds of Madness
Sealing the Deal
Spilling the Beans*

Demonic Contract
Anja's Secret
Daughter of Lions
Dragon's Blood
The Last Werewolf
Last Ama Princess
Transforming Rose
Lady Serra and the Draconian
Alys of Asgard
Phoenix Possessed
Sybil Deceived
The Pawn

Stone Heart
Of Sky and Sea

*COMING SOON

ABOUT THE AUTHOR

Catherine Banks is a USA Today bestselling fantasy author who writes in several fantasy subgenres and has multiple pseudonyms. She began writing fiction at only four years old and finished her first full-length novel at the age of fifteen. She is married to her soulmate and best friend, Avery, who she has two amazing children with. After her full-time job, she reads books, plays video games, and watches anime shows and movies with her family to relax. Although she has lived in Northern California her entire life, she dreams of traveling around the world. Catherine is also C.E.O. of Turbo Kitten Industries™, a company with many hats including being a book publisher and Etsy store full of nerdy fun.

facebook.com/catherinebanksauthor

twitter.com/catherineebanks

amazon.com/author/catherinebanks

bookbub.com/authors/catherine-banks